Cle

Recollections of Society

Vol. I

Anatiposi

Clementina Davies

Recollections of Society

Vol. I

Reprint of the original, first published in 1872.

1st Edition 2023 | ISBN: 978-3-38213-364-1

Anatiposi Verlag is an imprint of Outlook Verlagsgesellschaft mbH.

Verlag (Publisher): Outlook Verlag GmbH, Zeilweg 44, 60439 Frankfurt, Deutschland
Vertretungsberechtigt (Authorized to represent): E. Roepke, Zeilweg 44, 60439 Frankfurt, Deutschland
Druck (Print): Books on Demand GmbH, In de Tarpen 42, 22848 Norderstedt, Deutschland

RECOLLECTIONS OF SOCIETY

IN

FRANCE AND ENGLAND.

VOLUME I.

RECOLLECTIONS OF SOCIETY

IN

FRANCE AND ENGLAND.

BY

LADY CLEMENTINA DAVIES.

IN TWO VOLUMES.

VOL. I.

LONDON:
HURST AND BLACKETT, PUBLISHERS,
13, GREAT MARLBOROUGH STREET.
1872.

LONDON:
SAVILL, EDWARDS AND CO., PRINTERS, CHANDOS STREET,
COVENT GARDEN.

CONTENTS

OF

THE FIRST VOLUME.

CHAPTER I.

CHAPTER II.

CHAPTER III.

CHAPTER IV.

CHAPTER V.

CHAPTER VI.

CHAPTER VII.

CHAPTER VIII.

CHAPTER IX.

CHAPTER X.

CHAPTER XI.

CHAPTER XII.

CHAPTER XIII.

CHAPTER XIV.

CHAPTER XV.

CHAPTER I.

MY FAMILY—THE CHATEAU DE ST. GERMAIN—LORD MAURICE DRUMMOND—THE LITTLE TRIANON—PRACTICAL JOKES AT METZ—THE CHATEAU DE LUSSAN—"MANDRIN"—PRINCE TALLEYRAND—EGALITE—SINGULAR JOURNEY AND SUDDEN MARRIAGE—CAGLIOSTRO—VISIT OF LORD MAURICE DRUMMOND TO SCOTLAND—CURIOUS PEBBLE—LAST DAY OF QUEEN MARIE ANTOINETTE AT VERSAILLES—ROYAL FLIGHT—STRANGE SCENE IN THE GARDEN OF THE LUXEMBOURG—MARRIAGE OF MY PARENTS.

CHAPTER I.

SOME account of the family to which I belong will form a fitting introduction to my own more personal reminiscences.

Allied by the twofold tie of blood and gratitude to the Stuarts and through them to the Bourbons, the Chiefs of the Drummonds enjoyed the singular distinction of being proscribed and plundered at both the English Revolution of 1688, and the French Revolution of 1789. My ancestor, John, First Earl of Melfort, was Secretary of State to James II.; and, like his elder brother James, Fourth Earl of Perth, Lord Chancellor of Scotland, he accompanied his royal master in his flight to France. There, as everybody knows, the Château of St. Germain was generously assigned by Louis XIV. to the exiled King of England and his adherents for a residence.

The Earl of Melfort had a splendid suite of

apartments beneath those occupied by His Majesty; and, during a century afterwards, my immediate progenitors successively, though sometimes only occasionally, occupied those rooms consecrated to them by many historical and personal recollections, up to the time of the French Revolution of 1789, when they were driven from France. But, though domiciled in France, it was only as British subjects that they had resided there. A law was passed by the Parliament of Paris, in 1689, providing that, notwithstanding their enforced residence in France, all the followers of James II. were to be considered there, not as French subjects, but to all intents and purposes, and with regard to their legal acts,—such as marriages, &c.,—as subjects of His Britannic Majesty. And as my family had immense claims in Scotland, they were most careful in maintaining their rights as British subjects, though resident in France, and the fact of their nationality was always asserted by them on every important occasion: as, for example, when, in the time of Louis XVI. and Marie Antoinette, their Majesties stood sponsors for my uncle, born in France, and then, as always, they were described as "sujets de sa majesté Britannique."

My father, Lord Maurice Drummond, was the youngest son of James, Third Earl, Duke of Melfort.* Many were his recollections of Marie Antoinette in that bright time which preceded her unparalleled misfortunes. My father was then scarcely twenty years of age; and, remembering him as I well do, I can quite understand that he should have been considered extremely handsome in those days. Marie Antoinette, when at the bijou Château of Trianon, not only cultivated flowers, fished in the lake, milked cows, and invited her courtiers generally to share her pastoral pleasures, but she there acted in private theatricals, and always the part of a shepherdess or a soubrette. In the former character

* In order to simplify any question as to the apparent contradiction in speaking of the "Earls" of Perth and Melfort, and again of the "Dukes" of Perth and Melfort, it may be as well here to remind the reader that the Earls were created by James II. at St. Germains and after his abdication—namely, in 1695—Duke of Perth and Duke of Melfort, and these titles were confirmed to them in France by Louis XIV., at the same time that the other ducal titles of Berwick, Fitzjames, and Albemarle were confirmed to their several possessors.

she illustrated Rousseau's rural scenes in a way which, if he had beheld it, would have mitigated even that philosophic republican's well-known sarcasm on royal performers; and she so far overcame the educational or constitutional shyness of her royal husband in his earlier years as even to induce him to take a part on the stage.

There were, however, some inconveniences in the indulgence of Her Majesty's taste for theatricals, for my father has often told me that when she preferred to act her favourite rôle, he felt it most embarrassing to go through his part when it was necessary to *tutoyer* her. Marie Antoinette was happy then. Madame du Barry had shortly before presumed to call the future Louis XVI. "a lubberly boy;" but about the date of his proclamation as king, that monarch had suddenly awakened to a sense of his responsibility as a husband. And so little did Marie Antoinette—*la petite reine de vingt ans*—and her Court anticipate the coming storm of the Revolution that one of their favourite pastimes was a game called "Le Roi Détroné."

When, at fifteen years of age, Marie Antoinette had arrived in France as Dauphiness, she detected so much absurdity in the *ancien régime* formalities forced on her observance by the Duchesse de Noailles, the Grand Mistress of the Ceremonies, that she then and long afterwards spoke of that august personage by the sobriquet of *Madame Etiquette*. My grandmother belonged to the old Court, and clinging —as did most ladies of her age—to the time-honoured conventionalities of Versailles, she ventured to write to Marie Antoinette after her accession to the throne, on the impropriety, or imprudence, of any divergence on the part of Her Majesty from the traditional usages hitherto considered as part and parcel of royal etiquette in France. But the young Queen was intractable upon these points, as may be inferred from the following anecdote, the scene of which was the Bois de Boulogne.

My grandmother and my aunt, Lady Emilia Drummond, were one day there in attendance upon Her Majesty, being, like the rest of the more demure members of the Court, in open carriages. But the Queen was riding on a donkey, as indeed were various of her younger favourites. Suddenly, however, the whole cavalcade was stopped, for Marie Antoinette's donkey, having felt a sudden inclination to roll on the green turf, had thrown its royal rider, and she, being quite unhurt, remained seated on the ground, laughing immoderately. As soon, however, as she could command her countenance, she assumed a mock gravity, and, without attempting to rise from her lowly position, commanded that the Grand Mistress of the Ceremonies should at once be brought to her side. Nobody could imagine what Her Majesty was about either to say or do; but when the lady thus suddenly summoned to her presence, stood, in no good temper and with dignified aspect before her, she looked up and said—"Madame, I have sent for you that you may inform me as to the etiquette to be observed when a Queen of France and her donkey have both fallen—which of them is to get up first?" This odd question elicited smiles enough from the younger part of the Court in attendance; but—as was the case with many circumstances not dissimilar in their nature—its tendency was to make enemies for Marie Antoinette among not a few who, standing near the throne of France, were jealous for the maintenance of its dignity, and who—in their circumscribed view of human nature generally—were too apt to mistake the tokens of an innocent young heart, then free from care, for those of indecorous, not to say guilty levity.

Even in trifles, this "last Queen of France," as she has been pathetically called, could not conceal either her preferences or her distastes; in proof of which I may mention that one day when the Duke of Hamilton, who was dark, and my father, who was fair, were both in her presence, she asked some lady in attendance upon her—"To which of my Scotchmen do you yield the palm?" And then, without waiting for an answer to this unceremonious inquiry, she added—"For my own part, I prefer blue eyes."

It was an unprecedented circumstance to hear a Queen of France express herself thus freely, and it was still more strange to mark the desire for change, the love of adventure, which at that time took possession of the younger part of the noblesse at Versailles. This was most signally instanced in the voluntary flight of the young Marquis de Lafayette (a near connexion by marriage of the Duchesse de Noailles, the Grand Mistress of the Ceremonies above named), to fight for the cause of Independence in North America.

My father had at the age of fifteen years been noted for his love of fun both at the Court and in the camps of France. With regard to the latter, I may here at once say that in the reign of Louis XV., after the memorable battle so fatal to the Stuart cause (1746), my great-uncle, Lord Lewis Drummond, had returned to France, bringing back thither the regiment he had commanded at Culloden—one which had been raised by, and belonged to, the Duke of Perth, his cousin, and this regiment was afterwards purchased by the King of France, who gave a large sum for it, which was invested in the funds, and the interest secured in perpetuity to the head of our family.

The King of France also gave to any member of the family wishing to enter the French army, the privilege of choosing his own regiment. Another concession accorded them was that they should not be compelled to serve against England either by land or by sea. My uncle, James Lewis, Duke of Melfort, was, during the latter period of the long reign of Louis XV., Colonel of the regiment of Bassigny, and my father, when only fifteen years of age, commanded a company under his brother.

The regiment of Bassigny was at that time quartered at Metz. Many practical jokes were played by the officers there, not only on the inhabitants, but on each other. For example: All the young officers on their arrival there determined to astonish the people of the town, by pretending to bring the last Paris fashion, and wore large scarlet plumes in their hats when they were not in uniform. To their great amusement, they found that all the young men of the place mounted scarlet plumes as like theirs as possible; of course, after that the officers never wore them again, and the young men soon perceived that it was only a deception which had been practised upon them.

Shortly afterwards all the garrison officers were invited to a grand concert given by the gentlemen of the neighbourhood, and it was particularly mentioned that a lady would sing who was considered almost the finest singer in Europe. After they had been in the room for a short time, a very beautiful girl came forward;

but, to the astonishment of every one, she sang in a most antiquated style, making shakes and quavers at almost every note, and so ridiculous was her performance that they could not restrain their laughter, and left the room, only returning as soon as they thought they could listen with proper attention to the other singers. Some very good singing now went on for about two hours, when the beautiful "prima donna" was again brought forward. They hardly knew what to do, they could not help greeting her with ill-suppressed signs of merriment; but, to their surprise, she sang this time in the most perfect good taste and style; so that they could scarcely believe it was the same person who had sung at the beginning of the concert. They applauded to the utmost; and she then came forward in a timid and graceful manner, saying to the officers—"Gentlemen, I think we have made a return for the scarlet plumes." They were all much amused with the jest, and charmed with the beautiful "prima donna."

My father frequently went to the soirées given by the Baronne de Rastignac, where cards formed the chief amusement. One night he remained late and had won a good deal of money. After returning home, he had not long been in bed, when he dreamt he was still at the Baronne's, winning everything he played for. Waking up, he resolved to return to the card-table; he knew he should be in time, for they always played till broad daylight; so he went as soon as possible, and did actually win the whole night. He again returned home and went to bed, and slept very soundly for two or three hours, but it was parade morning, and his servant soon came to wake him. Getting out of bed, he went straight to the drawer where he had a vague idea he had put rouleaus of gold, though not quite sure that it was more than a dream; when to his great satisfaction he found the gold was indeed there. He had gone so late to bed and was so sleepy, that in his hurry to dress he put on with his uniform the cravat he had just taken off. On the way to parade he discovered his mistake, and pushed the ends of it inside the collar of his coat. A friend of his, Captain McMahon, an Irishman, whose family had also followed the unfortunate James II. in exile, and who was in garrison at Metz, came up to him, saying, "Why, you have forgotten your uniform cravat;" at the same time taking hold of the little point of the necktie which my father had tried to conceal. The latter replied in a tone of vexation, "Don't do that again, McMahon; I don't want it noticed," and not pleased with the other's manner, added, "If you do it again I'll not stand it." McMahon only laughed, and jokingly again pulled out the end of the offending cravat. My father just whispered something to him, and when parade was over, it was observed they had both disappeared. In the duel which followed, my father wounded Captain McMahon seriously, and a rumour soon got about that one of the English officers had killed the other. My father was in great alarm, dreading lest he had really killed Captain McMahon, and lost no time in starting off for "le pays de la Reine," which was then a sanctuary. He stayed at a farmhouse, remaining there till able to correspond with his brother and Colonel, explaining the circumstances, and waiting anxiously to learn whether McMahon was dead or recovering. To his delight, in the course of about a month he received the intelligence that he was recovering fast, and he immediately returned to Metz. The moment he arrived, his brother put him under arrest.

He, with the officers who used to come to see him, thought it would be a good joke for him to go to the play dressed as a lady; and with the assistance of the Marquis and the Marquise de la Fare, he managed to do so. He was so fair, so handsome, and so young, that when thus dressed he looked, notwithstanding his height, an elegant girl. His hair, which was very long, according to the fashion of the day, was dressed out to the best advantage; they boldly took him to the theatre, and placed him in the box next to his Colonel's. Nothing in his equipment had been forgotten; my father had a fan, which he held up and shyly looked over at his brother, who was wondering who this beautiful girl might be, and kept staring at her, my father always screening his face with his fan and flirting in a most unconscionable manner. The consequence was that the Duke, who was not a married man, and admired this "new beauty," whom he was quite sure he had never seen before in Metz, passed into the Marquis de la Fare's box, to find out who she was. "The young lady" turned her back upon him as he entered, and held her fan in such a way that he could not possibly see her face, she pretending to be very much interested in the performance. The Duke of Melfort determined to remain in the box till they should leave the theatre, when the Marquis offered his arm to this fair girl to conduct her to the carriage, and the Duke could not do otherwise than conduct the Marquise. He asked her some few questions, but she had been told what replies to make, adding she would be happy to see him the following day and introduce him; he then, making both ladies a very low bow, retired.

The next morning my father went in uniform to meet his brother at la Marquise de la Fare's. The Duke was at first very angry, and ordered him into arrest again; but by the intervention of his friends it was finally arranged that he should set off immediately for the Château de Lussan. The laugh throughout the regiment was against the poor Colonel. My father lost no time in going off to Lussan to join his mother, his brothers, and his sisters.

Lussan was a very large château, built in

the form of a quadrangle, and carried with it the title of Comte to whoever was the possessor. The estate, although very extensive, produced very little in rents; there were fourteen villages belonging to it, and immense forests—le Bois de Ruffe, le Bois de Fans, and several others. A singular remnant of feudalism prevailed there; my grandmother had to sit in the Court of Justice and give judgment, and even had the power of life and death over the inhabitants of the villages. There were many Protestants among them; indeed almost half the population were of that persuasion, and she used to have many discussions with her chaplain, always opposing his views about her Protestant "subjects," whom he called heretics.

One day, when they were quietly sitting at breakfast, the steward came to say that "Mandrin" and his band were in sight. This Mandrin was a sort of French Rob-Roy. My grandmother immediately gave orders that everything should be prepared for them; that is, plenty to eat and plenty to drink, in a large and comfortable room. She had had more than one visit from them before, and had always treated them with the same hospitality. After eating and drinking and remaining till it was nearly dark, Mandrin desired the steward to return his best thanks, and went away without taking anything whatever. This was very different from the course he pursued where he was ill-treated; then he took horses and cattle, or whatever he could get, and it would have required a great many men to successfully oppose him and his band.

My grandmother and her family remained at Lussan for some time, when they went to Paris. Prince Talleyrand and my uncle, the Abbé Lord Charles Edward, pursued their studies together at the séminaire; and the former spent all his vacations with my grandmother and uncles and aunts either at the Château de St. Germain or at Lussan. He had been shamefully used by his parents. On account of the misfortune of his clubfoot, he was deprived of his rights and all the estates which, as eldest son, he would have had, and forced against his will to become a priest. He never forgave this, and never went near them.

One day Prince Talleyrand and my father went to the Colisée. This was a promenade where the nobility and persons of position only were admitted, and without an introduction no one could go in. The gate-keeper did not hold Prince Talleyrand in anything like the respect due to the future great diplomatist of Europe, and my father was so young and so fair that, notwithstanding his uniform, he thought Prince Talleyrand's companion was a young lady in disguise, and cried out—"Vous ne pouvez pas passer, Mademoiselle," and held the gate closed. Talleyrand, thinking it an excellent joke, with a most serious expression turned to my father, saying—"Tu vois, ma mie, tu ne peux pas entrer." Upon this the gate-keeper came boldly forward to my father, to interpose his stern authority, when my father, taking his sword, gave him such a thrashing with the flat side of it, that capering about in pain he cried out—"C'est assez, c'est assez—ah passez, Monsieur, ah passez, Monsieur." Talleyrand was perfectly delighted, although I was told he did not even smile.

In 1783 my father was some years older than in his merry days at Metz, and, being in favour at the Court of Louis XVI. and

Marie Antoinette, united with his brother, the Duke of Melfort, in so placing the Scottish territorial claims of our family under the favourable notice of the King and Queen of France, that their Majesties desired their Minister, M. d'Adhémar, to do all that was requisite in order to convince the British Cabinet of their interest in the case.

At one time it was the intention of my uncle, the Duke of Melfort, to proceed immediately to England, there to represent his own interests*; but his cousin, the Vicomte de Melfort (having heard of this intention, and knowing that the Duke's approaching marriage made him just then anxious not to leave France), obtained a power of attorney from him which would enable him in England to act in his stead respecting his claims.

The Duc de Chartres (afterwards the Duc d'Orléans, better known as Egalité) had invited the Vicomte de Melfort to accompany him on a visit to the Prince of Wales, in London, and thither accordingly they started.

* James Drummond, of Lundin, was believed to be dead before the Drummond estates were restored.

While taking advantage of the hospitality of the Prince of Wales the Vicomte de Melfort met most of the English beauties then at St. James's, who rivalled each other, in the apartments of the maids-of-honour and the ladies-in-waiting. But, in the eyes of the Vicomte de Melfort, Lady Caroline B——y outshone them all. It was therefore with no regret that, still ostensibly occupied in pressing on the family claims temporarily represented by him, he found himself detained in England for six months; and at the end of that time followed the Duc de Chartres to France.

Not long afterwards, he was one day on duty as Captain of the Garde du Corps at Versailles, when he was summoned to receive some friends of his who had just arrived from England, and he was delighted and surprised to find that they were no other than Lady Caroline and her brother, Lord B——e.

"And now," exclaimed the latter, "we are come, dear Vicomte de Melfort, in the hope that under your escort and protection we may see all the wonders of Versailles and Paris."

They were not disappointed. For six weeks the fascinating Lady Caroline and her brother were everywhere; sometimes in the midst of pastoral scenes *à la Watteau*, acted by the Queen and her Court at the Little Trianon, sometimes at a royal reception, where Marie Antoinette, *en grande tenue*, at Versailles, shone resplendent as the chief centre of her own brilliant Court, conspicuous amid whom were the lovely Princesse de Lamballe, the graceful Duchesse de Polignac, and the gay Comte d'Artois, the favourite brother-in-law of Her Majesty; sometimes in Paris, at the Palais Royal, where, as guests of the Duc and Duchesse de Chartres, they had an opportunity of hearing the celebrated Madame de Genlis read her own verses, or play upon the harp; sometimes at the theatre, where the Queen herself would laugh at the wit of Beaumarchais in *Figaro*, never thinking how deadly in its political influence on the people was the satire that lurked beneath the humour of that brilliant comedy.

At the end of those six weeks Lord B——e said that he must forthwith return to England, for the Derby Day at Epsom was at hand, and he had enormously heavy bets dependent upon the race; wherefore he and his sister bade farewell to Versailles.

Many there regretted the necessity of this departure, but none so much as the Vicomte de Melfort, who asked and obtained permission to accompany the travellers on the few first stages of their journey towards the French coast. They had not, however, proceeded more than ten miles on their way when the carriage broke down; and this too at a spot near which was neither post-house, carpenter, nor smith, and where they could procure no other conveyance.

Lord B——e was distracted; for he had postponed his departure to the last possible hour, and had not a moment to lose so as to get to England in time for the Derby.

Almost at his wits' end, he turned to the Vicomte de Melfort, and exclaimed, "I must be off; stay here and take care of my sister while I go and find another carriage." He then mounted one of the unharnessed horses, and rode off. But by the time he reached the nearest post-house he was so much further on his journey, and the time before the Derby was so much the shorter that, instead of going back himself with the carriage for his sister, he sent it by a man, who was also entrusted by him with a hastily-written note to explain that an hour's more delay would be extremely disastrous to him, but that he trusted to the Vicomte for the safety of his sister.

The Derby was soon over, and Lord B——e returned to France; for Lady Caroline had not arrived in England, nor had she returned to Versailles. But her brother, knowing where he had left her, had no great difficulty in finding both her and his friend. This was a very embarrassing circumstance, and at first he felt at a loss how to act. Should he call out his sister's admirer, and stop the tongue of scandal by shooting the Vicomte? Irishmen were fond of fighting in those days; but happily there was a more pleasant alternative, which the Vicomte de Melfort preferred; and the three fellow-travellers suddenly re-appeared in Paris, where a marriage was solemnized at the Embassy, between the Vicomte de Melfort and Lady Caroline B——y; after which the bride and bridegroom, and the brother of the bride, again set off on their journey, and in due course of time arrived in London. The Vicomte meanwhile had written a very humble letter to his father, the Comte de Melfort, saying that he was sure of his paternal pardon for having married without his consent, since his bride possessed not only beauty and rank, but money. And indeed, no sooner did Lady Caroline appear before her father-in-law than her husband was forgiven.

Later on in these pages it will be seen whether or not this marriage proved a happy one. That it owed its origin to the Derby was only too much in accordance with the spirit of the times, for the rage for gambling was then all powerful not only in England, but also in France, and particularly at Versailles, where it pervaded society to such a degree that there was scarcely any event of either private or political importance which was not in some sort influenced by it.

Gamblers are proverbially superstitious, and thus a way was paved there for professors of the marvellous, not the least of whom was Cagliostro, whose now well-known diamond necklace conspiracy helped eventually to precipitate the downfall of Marie Antoinette.

Even my grandmother, though a *grande dame* of the *ancien régime*, believed in Cagliostro. That renowned seer, albeit of Hebrew extraction and a whilom student of Arabic and other strange lore, had just appeared in Paris under the protection of the Cardinal Prince de Rohan. According to current credulity—at that time, a hundred years ago, he caused a sort of epidemic—his occult powers were so great that he could foretell the future and also describe the past.

The Vicomtesse de Beauharnais (afterwards the Empress Joséphine), was at that time in Paris, and there frequently visited my grandmother and my aunts. One day it happened that being together, and each one of them having her own separate anxiety, they determined to visit Cagliostro, in order to hear what Fate might severally have in store for them. Upon reaching his abode, they were ushered into a large room, the furniture and curtains of which were all of dark green velvet; and, after waiting there for a few minutes, they were conducted into a smaller apartment, which was not only exquisitely fitted up, but brilliantly illuminated, although out of doors it was still broad daylight. Almost dazzled by this artificial light, the effect of which was enhanced, perhaps, by its contrast with the subdued tone of colouring which pervaded the apartment into which they had first been shown, they found themselves in presence of Cagliostro himself. He was a rather tall man, with a somewhat Jewish cast of countenance. He wore a loose black velvet gown, richly embroidered; and, as his visitors entered, he rose, bowed, and then immediately passed to the opposite side of a large table standing in the centre of the room, and covered with enormous cards, and remained silent for some time.

Madame de Beauharnais was anxious about her son, Eugène, then a mere boy, the future Viceroy of Italy. Cagliostro assured her of his present safety, and then added—"But, stay, Madame la Vicomtesse, I have something more to say to you. An extraordinary destiny lies before you. You will be more than Queen of France, but you will die on a *fumier*."*

Madame de Beauharnais was exceedingly startled by this announcement on the part of Cagliostro, and the more so because in her childhood at Martinique, and under circumstances of which if he had any knowledge it could only be of an occult nature, a negress, it is said, had likewise foretold to her that she would be more than Queen of France. To my grandmother, and to each of the other ladies present, Cagliostro foretold events which literally, and without any agency of theirs, came to pass; and this continued to impress my grandmother with a sense of his power, and in after-years she expressed her convictions of its reality to the Comtesse de Valmont. The Comtesse said that she also had strange cause to share that conviction; for at one time when her husband was in Spain, and a sudden cessation of all correspondence on his part caused her great

---

* Malmaison, the residence to which the Empress Joséphine retired after her divorce, and where she died, was built upon what had been the refuse heap of the stables which formerly stood there.

anxiety, she, then residing in Paris, had gone to Cagliostro to ascertain the cause of her husband's silence. She was received by him in a small room, opening through a glass door into a conservatory filled with beautiful flowers. He conducted her thither, and being requested by him to pluck a flower, she gathered a white rose. Inhaling the perfume of this flower, she returned to the sofa in the room adjoining the conservatory, but scarcely had she done so when she began to feel drowsy, and was soon overpowered with sleep. From this repose, however, she suddenly started with a scream, alarmed by a vision which had appeared before her with all the vividness of reality. She had seen her husband lying on a bed as if recently wounded; and he had told her that he had been engaged in a duel, provoked by political animosity. Cagliostro was perfectly well aware of all that had been revealed to her in this strange sleep, for while under its influence, she had talked to her husband as though in his actual presence; and for her own part, so strong was the impression made upon her mind that she could not satisfy herself whether all she had seen and heard said had occurred really, or was only a dream.

Cagliostro explained to her that it was by the force of his mesmeric influence that her mind had been transported; but she was so deeply impressed by a conviction of the actual truth of all she had witnessed, that upon returning home, she ordered immediate preparations to be made for her journey into Spain. Night and day she travelled thither, in the utmost anxiety, allowing herself no rest on the long journey; and when she reached her destination, she found that her husband really had been wounded, while everything else had happened precisely as it had appeared in her strange vision.

In 1784, James Drummond, afterwards created Baron Perth, obtained the Scotch estates which my uncle had claimed. As soon as he was in possession of Drummond Castle he invited my father to pay him a visit, which he did, and was very much pleased with the reception he met with.

After having remained with him for a short time, my father visited Lord Adam Gordon and Drummond of Blair Drummond, very old friends of our family, with whom they had always kept up a correspondence while at the Château of St. Germain.

He thus spent a few months very agreeably, and then returned to France for his brother's marriage, who had been prevented from going to Drummond Castle with my father on account of his approaching nuptials.

My father remained in France for two or three years, dividing his time between Versailles, Paris, and St. Germain, and entered fully into all the gaieties of the Court.

In 1788 my father went to pay a second visit to Drummond Castle, and my aunt, Lady Emily, accompanied him. Assembled there was a collection of the beauties of the time, conspicuous among whom were Lady Charlotte Campbell, Miss Campbell, and Miss Robertson, so remarkable for their beauty, which lasted for so many years, and whom we shall meet again.

After remaining at Drummond Castle for some weeks, my father, with Lord and Lady Perth, went to the sea-side, and during their stay there a very singular occurrence took place.

As they were one day walking on the beach, Lady Perth's little daughter, who was amusing herself in picking up pebbles, suddenly brought one for her mother to look at, the appearance of which was enough to cause a start of surprise; for on this stone—though no chisel nor any instrument whatever could have touched it—was represented a head surmounted with a casque of Liberty, such as that the sight of which subsequently became only too familiar in France as worn by the goddess in whose name so many crimes were committed. Lady Perth looked with astonishment at Nature's curious tracing of this remarkable pebble, and gave it to my father. Not quite unprophetic at that moment was Lady Perth of events which were then only just beginning to cast their shadows before them in France; and yet it seemed that she would, if she could, have saved the kinsman to whom she spoke from the serious vicissitudes awaiting him on his return thither, for in a moment afterwards she urged him with much energy to remain in Scotland, instead of returning to France.

In 1789, hardly a year afterwards, the Assembly of the States-General took place;

the chronology of the French Revolution began, and upon the 6th of October in the same year the King and Queen were brought, under circumstances well-known, by an insurgent mob from Versailles to Paris.

The Tuileries had been uninhabited for more than a century when Louis XVI. and Marie Antoinette were compelled, by their disaffected subjects, to take up their abode there. Suddenly the regal splendour of Versailles had passed away for ever, and with it all the gaiety and animation which had previously distinguished the Queen as the most brilliant woman of her own Court.

It was upon the morning of her involuntary departure from Versailles that Marie Antoinette first appeared in a new character before her people, for the noble heroism of her subsequent conduct in face of danger then almost unexpectedly manifested itself as she stood dauntlessly upon the balcony, overlooking the marble court of the palace in which the surging multitude had assembled.

She stood perfectly motionless, but in an attitude both noble and composed. Her dress was white, and her head being bare, her fair hair, at that moment of consternation dishevelled and unpowdered, floated about her. "The enraged people, however, were not softened by the sight of woe in all its majesty," as said the Marquis de Lavalette, who further declared that even at that moment Marie Antoinette appeared like a victim.

The Château of the Tuileries was more a prison than a palace to the ill-fated King and Queen of France: and thence at last (within a fortnight after Robespierre was elected public accuser for the Tribunal of the Seine) they determined to escape.

My father aided in the scheme of that well-contrived but eventually frustrated flight to Varennes, which took place on the 21st day of June, 1791. Indelibly engraven on the heart of everybody concerned in it was the fatal evening when Louis XVI. and Marie Antoinette, their two surviving children, their sister, Madame Elizabeth, and a few of their still faithful followers, all in various disguises, stole out separately from the Tuileries, having beforehand agreed on a place of meeting, near at hand, not likely to be suspected.

With every successive league interposed between themselves and Paris, the Royal fugitives believed themselves to be safer and safer. That anxious night-journey, so well arranged that its successful issue seemed certain, led them through a country which then, at Midsummer time, still looked fair and fertile, though it was so soon to be deluged with the best blood of France. But, alas! upon the morning of the day which it was hoped would have seen the King and Queen of France safe beyond the frontier of that kingdom, then theirs only in name, they were recognised at St. Ménéhould by the postmaster's son, Jean Baptiste Drouet, the future regicide, and on reaching Varennes, the secret of their identity having been meanwhile betrayed, they were detained at the house of M. Saussé, the Mayor of the Commune. Bystanders there insulted misfortune in the person of Louis XVI., and it was then that Marie Antoinette, fired by indignation, exclaimed, "Since you recognise your King, speak, if you speak at all, with the respect due to him." The cowardly mob shrank back on hearing these few words pronounced in a tone of indignant remonstrance, or rather cowered before the real majesty of their speaker, and the King then implored the people around him to save the Queen and her children. But no, it was not to be. They were detained until a decree of the National Assembly concerning them could arrive from Paris. Hour after hour passed, a whole night of despair, but of despair borne with dignified calmness; and when at last the decree came, ordering the instant return of the Royal fugitives to Paris, the Queen's hair had turned grey.

For my father's share in having attempted to save the King and Queen, he was eventually cast into the prison of St. Yon, near Sotteville, in Normandy, where he remained for eleven dreary months, during which the horrors of his incarceration were intensified in proportion to the fast-increasing number of his fellow-captives—who were allowed only black bread, sometimes full of worms, to eat, and dirty water, sometimes putrid, to drink. He occupied a room, in company with other prisoners, and as most of these were of noble birth, and therefore opposed to the Republicanism then raging in France, they were made to pass their nights and days in the presence of a treacherous ruffian, who had received orders from his sanguinary employers to draw them into conversation, in which he abused Robespierre and his myrmidons, hoping that he might elicit in reply from some of the gentlemen around him words which, being reported, would inevitably consign those who had uttered them to the guillotine at once.

The King's next brother, Monsieur (afterwards Louis XVIII.), had effected his escape beyond the French frontier, having fled from Paris on the same day that their Majesties had started for Varennes, but by a different route from theirs; and the palace of the Luxembourg, formerly occupied by him, was converted after his departure from it into a prison. The miseries and massacres in the prisons of Paris in those bad times are too notorious to need any detailed account of them here, but still it is impossible to pass over the recollections of my family respecting them without glancing for a moment at the strange scene then daily enacted in the Garden of the Luxembourg.

There, day after day, did a multitude of

unhappy women assemble in the hope of seeing their husbands, their lovers, their brothers, their sons, in short, the one being in the world severally most dear to each of them, at the windows of the prison. Some of these women had until quite lately been leaders of fashion in the brilliant society of the Court and of the Faubourg St. Germain. But now, though hitherto unused to aught but luxury, they were dauntless in braving all weather, and though the rain might pour, or the air freeze, or the heat be intolerable, they would stand for hours waiting and watching for the merest chance of receiving some momentary look or token of remembrance.

It was no unusual thing for some of these faithful women to faint with fatigue as they stood there, and while all of them of necessity wore humble clothing, not a few would assume the garb of beggars, in which disguise a child might be carried without raising too much suspicion—a child to be held up, should the mother's tearful eyes rest but one moment on the father, who, for anything she could tell to the contrary, might the next hour be led forth from his prison to the scaffold.

It was not until after the execution of Robespierre that my father was released from captivity; but notwithstanding the tyrant's fall, Paris was no safe place for those who had formerly been known there as Royalists, and therefore he remained at Sotteville, in Normandy, where he was soon afterwards married to my mother as a *citoyen* to a *citoyenne.*

CHAPTER II.

TALLEYRAND—RETURN OF MY FAMILY TO THE CHÂTEAU DE ST. GERMAIN—FAMILY VICISSITUDES—UTRECHT AT THE BEGINNING OF THE NINETEENTH CENTURY—THE BIRTH OF MY BROTHER, THE EARL OF PERTH—ARRIVAL OF MY FAMILY AND MYSELF IN EDINBURGH—SIR HUMPHREY DAVY.

CHAPTER II.

MY parents continued to reside at Sotteville during the progress of all the later stages of the French Revolution. At last my father's old friend, Talleyrand, wrote to him, saying that it would now be quite safe for him to return to his former domicile in the Château de St. Germain. I myself knew Talleyrand well in the later years of his life; and as in the course of my acquaintance with him I had reason to form quite a different view of his character from the one generally received by the world, I will here remind the reader of some few facts concerning his early life.

Charles Maurice Talleyrand de Périgord was born in the month of February, 1751. His father was the representative of an illustrious house; for the principality of Chalais had existed for eight centuries in the family of Périgord, whose prefix Talleyrand (anciently written *Tailleran*) is supposed to have originated from a sobriquet derived from the words *tailler les rangs*, — "Cut through the ranks."

The mother of Charles Maurice was much admired at the Court of Versailles during the reign of Louis XV. But finding that her maternal duties were incompatible with those appertaining to her position in the royal household, she sent him, her eldest son, to be reared in a distant province; and when, some ten or twelve years afterwards, he returned to her, he had become an incurable cripple. Talleyrand himself, when speaking in later years of his infirmity, attributed it to a fall from a tree; but, whatever its cause, the consequences of it exercised a marked influence over his character and career through life. For, as a cripple, he was unfit for the army, and was therefore consigned to the priesthood; and by the same family council which decreed his dedication to the Church, it was decided that his younger brother (afterwards known as the Duc de Périgord) should be considered the elder. Deprived thus of his birthright, Talleyrand was early placed in antagonism to fate. The cynicism of his wit was developed in proportion as his talents were cultivated by his ecclesiastical education; and in course of time it was by a *bon mot* uttered in the presence of his friend and patroness, Madame Dú Barry, that he first achieved ecclesiastical promotion: for, being one day rallied by her as to his silence when in her society, "Hélas, Madame," he sighed, "je faisais une réflexion bien triste: Paris est une ville dans laquelle il est bien plus aisé d'avoir des femmes que des abbayes!"

This *mot* was rewarded by a benefice; and the Abbé de Périgord rose so rapidly in his profession, or rather in Court favour, that in 1789 he was consecrated Bishop of Autun. "If he thought like a deist he preached like a saint;" and when, in the month of July, 1790, the first federal fête took place on the Champ de Mars, it was he who, robed in tricolor episcopal vestments, stood upon the mighty altar erected there, and attended by three hundred priests, blessed all the eighty-three departmental flags of France, whilst the pious King Louis XVI. swore, with his hand outstretched towards heaven, to maintain the Constitution decreed by the National Assembly and accepted by him.

Talleyrand was, previous to this, the friend of Mirabeau, and was united with him in the hope of founding in France a constitutional government. But when, in 1791, Mirabeau died, and the royal flight to Varennes was frustrated, he became, like every one else, convinced that the monarchy was lost.

Besides his regard for my father, of which he was always ready to give proofs, there was, as I subsequently discovered, another link connecting Prince Talleyrand with my family. Many years afterwards, "the prince of diplomatists" told me that at a period before the Revolution, and therefore antecedent to his own ultimate secularization and consequent power to marry, he was devotedly attached to my aunt, Lady Emilia Drummond. Upon this point I shall say more hereafter; so suffice it to add, that, availing themselves of Talleyrand's suggestion, my parents, accompanied by my grandmother and my aunts, at once returned to the Château de St. Germain.

Talleyrand himself had come back from

exile to Paris in 1794, and there been made a member of the National Institute. In 1797 the Administration of Foreign Affairs was confided to him and his power augmented. At that time the Palais Royal was the scene of sedition and out-of-door oratory. Who could have foreseen that Egalité himself would so soon fall a victim on the guillotine, to the spirit of that Republicanism he had helped to invoke?

I was the last of my family whose birth took place in the Château de St. Germain. The room in which I was born (on the 21st of November, in the fourth year of the first French Republic) was very large, with an immense window opening on a balcony just over the principal entrance to the palace. A statue of the Goddess of Liberty, or rather of the celebrated Madame Tallien, stood on the pavement in front of the room in which, I was told, I first saw the light. There were other objects within and without the Château which have left an indelible impression on my memory, for at St. Germain the earlier years of my childhood were passed. The apartments occupied for a century by my family were, as I have said, under those which had belonged to the King. They consisted of about fifteen or sixteen rooms, and formed the *entresol.* They were large, and well furnished, each room opening into a corridor which ran round the entire Château. The furniture, covered with damask, was ornamented in the Louis XIV. style. The coverlet on my grandmother's bed was, I remember, of splendid red brocade, embroidered most richly in gold with the Royal Arms of England; for it had served as the covering of the horse on which Prince Charles Edward rode at the battle of Culloden; and I may here mention, as a curious fact, that at Culloden the unfortunate Prince wore the Drummond, and not the Stuart tartan. The family pictures in the drawing-room were numerous, and there was also a painting of the Blind Homer dictating his poems to a boy. In the bedroom where I was born, there was a mirror over the fireplace, surmounted by a beautiful Correggio, a Sleeping Child, so exquisitely painted that if you gazed at it for any length of time you could not help fancying you saw the pillow rise and fall with the child's breathing; at least so it appeared to me as a child.

Most visitors to France are familiar with the external appearance of the Château de St. Germain, and will therefore easily recall to mind the gloomy aspect of the five-storied building, its massive five façades, its paved courtyard, and its pentangular fosse. The latter, three-quarters of a century ago, was a moat filled with water, and stocked with fine fish. I well remember the carp, which (like those still at Chantilly and Versailles) were almost tame, whilst some of them were so old that my father told me that one bore in his gills a ticket which proved him to be over two hundred years of age.*

On one side of the Château was the parterre where, many years after, I used to walk, thinking of the strange vicissitudes which this royal residence had undergone since

* Some of the carp at Versailles are proved to have attained an almost incredible longevity, by silver rings which, passed through their gills, are inscribed not only with the date when the ring was so inserted, but with the name of the courtier who inserted it.

the far bygone age when King Robert, the Crusader, founded it, or Henri IV. rebuilt it, or Louis XIV. added to it, and then forsook it because from its windows he could see St. Denis, the burial-place of his ancestors—destined to be his own.

That burial-place had not long since been torn open by sacrilegious hands, and the embalmed occupants of its vaults and coffins exposed to the view of an impious mob, at the time when I was born. But the noble forest, where Bourbon kings were for centuries wont to hunt, still stretched out before me, and out of it wolves would sometimes prowl almost close to the Parterre gates, notwithstanding the sentries who paced up and down and there kept guard.*

In 1800 both Lord Perth and my uncle, James Lewis, Duke of Melfort, died,—the latter in Spain, where he had taken refuge

* In more recent years the Château of St. Germain has undergone various vicissitudes, it having been at one time used as a flour-store, and at another as a prison. But for this, Napoleon III. would have restored the old apartments, so long used by my family, to my brother, the present Earl of Perth. The rooms, therefore, above described, are still standing, but unfurnished.

with some of his Spanish relations on the outbreak of the troubles in France. The daughter of the first Earl, Duke of Melfort, married the Count de Castel Blanco, and of her two grandaughters, one married the Infant of Spain, and the other the Duc de Lyria.

The heir of the Duke of Melfort, since he left no child, was Lord Charles Edward Drummond, my father's elder brother, who, as an "aristocrat" and a Roman Catholic priest, had fled from France during the Reign of Terror; but in 1800, it was so long since he had been heard of, that my father, supposing that he was dead, determined at once to proceed to England.

Accompanied by my mother, my sisters, and myself, my father arrived in London, and there he was most kindly received by the widowed Lady Perth (who then lived in Grosvenor Square), and also by her daughter, the child whom the reader will remember as picking up pebbles on the seashore, but who had now grown up to womanhood. With regard, however, to the object of his journey to England, Lady Perth said to my father—"You are quite mistaken in supposing that your brother, the Abbé, is dead; he has given us more annoyance than I can possibly tell you; but at last we are at rest, for he was forced to leave England, and we have not heard of him for a long time."

My father was, nevertheless, advised to put in his claim, and, not to speak more here of the missing Abbé, his brother, and other family circumstances connected with the property, I need only add that a pecuniary arrangement having been entered into between my father and Miss Drummond's guardians, we returned to St. Germain.

During the subsequent war time, it was so difficult to keep up a correspondence with England, and the arrival in France of remittances was so uncertain, that my father appealed to his old friend, Talleyrand, then Minister for Foreign Affairs, on the subject, and it was at length determined that we should again proceed to England, but by way of Holland, and under another name.

I remember well, during that journey, staying for a short time at Utrecht, where the dwellings and shops of the Moravians were placed quite close to one another, and built in a line. They formed, indeed, a true community, for all the money received by them in trade was divided equally among all the shopkeepers; but the dampness of the place, and the rough manners of its population, were such as to make me think of it in after-years as best described by Voltaire's well-known alliteration—"*Canaux, canards, et canaille!*"

Upon our arrival in London, we found that it was still uncertain whether my uncle, the Abbé, was alive or dead. My aunt, Lady Emilia Drummond, had for some time past been the guest of Lady Perth, in Grosvenor Square. It was my father's intention soon to take my mother, my only surviving sister, and myself to Scotland, there to visit various old friends of his family. Two events, however, detained us in London—my brother, the present Earl of Perth, was born, and my sister died.

As soon as we could recover a little from this sad loss we went to Edinburgh. A short time after our arrival there I was taken to a school kept by Miss Playfair, sister to the professor of that name. While under her care, I well remember often seeing Sir Humphry Davy, nor can I forget an occasion on which Sir Humphrey was seated on a sort of throne, when a laurel crown was placed on his head by Mrs. Apreece, to whom he was subsequently married, one of the celebrated literary ladies then resident in the "Modern Athens."

My father, however, was still so much depressed on account of the recent death of my sister, that he resolved to remove me from school, so that he might have more of my company, as at that time my mother was absorbed by her attention to my little brother, and I, at a very early age, began to go into society with my father.

CHAPTER III.

HOLYROOD HOUSE—THE COMTE D'ARTOIS—EDINBURGH THEATRICALS — CATALANI — MRS. JORDAN — MRS. SIDDONS IN PRIVATE AND IN PUBLIC — "MISSED A POINT" — JOHN KEMBLE—THE "QUEEN'S ASSEMBLY"—MASCULINE *versus* FEMININE INFLUENCE—SCOTCH BEAUTIES—SIR WALTER SCOTT—SIR WILLIAM CUMMING GORDON AND MISS GRACE BAILLIE—A FANCY DRESS.

CHAPTER III.

I WAS about fifteen years old, when in Edinburgh I had the opportunity of meeting some very remarkable personages of that day.

The Comte d'Artois (afterwards Charles X.) was then at Holyrood House, and thither my father frequently took me. In his early days at Versailles and in Paris he had been well acquainted with this, the youngest and favourite brother-in-law of Marie Antoinette; and many, though now mournful by contrast, were their common reminiscences of bright days at the Little Trianon and elsewhere. The Comte d'Artois was still handsome at the time of his residence at Holyrood, but a dark shadow had fallen on his life; for it was at a then still recent date of his long exile from France that he had lost Madame de Polastron, the one woman whom he had loved so well that by the side of her death-bed he had declared to her confessor, the Abbé (afterwards Cardinal) de Latil, that she should never have a successor in his affections.

In attendance upon the French prince at Edinburgh were several of the former courtiers of Versailles, though all more or less changed in appearance during the long years of their exile; and amongst them was the well-known Comte de Coigny, who had still a very fine face, but who had grown so fat and gouty that he was no longer recognizable in figure as the same man my father had known before the Revolution.

Private theatricals were much in fashion in Edinburgh at the time to which I now refer; and chiefly distinguished then for histrionic talent amongst amateur performers was a Mr. Beauclerc, introduced by the late Lord Fife. Mr. Beauclerc was such a perfect actor that Mrs. Siddons said he would have made a fortune on the public stage.

Catalani, Mrs. Jordan, Mrs. Siddons, John Kemble, and Henry Siddons were all in Edinburgh at the period to which my recollections now carry me back. Catalani's voice was still splendid, and almost every Sunday we used to meet her at the house of Lord Fingall, an old friend of my father; and when she sang in church the crowd was so great that it was not only difficult to find standing room, but many persons invariably fainted. In private society this great *cantatrice* was much liked for her agreeable manners. Mrs. Jordan was also at Edinburgh, and there I had an opportunity of seeing her off as well as on the stage, for when she was about to act it was advertised that tickets were to be obtained from her personally at her own house, and thither—like numbers of other people—went my father and myself to buy them. It is long since that time, but I have still a vivid remembrance of Mrs. Jordan as she then appeared.

She had very pretty features and beautiful eyes, but was marked with the small-pox. In manner she was animated, and her acting was most lively and charming, but she was rather too old and too fat for some of her favourite parts, and more especially for that of "The Romp," which at that date she was performing in Edinburgh.

To see Mrs. Siddons on the stage was my great desire. She and John Kemble had both left off acting for some years in London, but they were so pleased with the reception they met with in Edinburgh that they promised to give two public performances there, and my eagerness to be present upon one of these occasions was increased after having met them, in company with my father, one evening at the house of Lady Drummond.

My father, who is mentioned in a previous page as having acted with Marie Antoinette at Trianon and Versailles, was charmed with them; and the more so because they both critically understood the beauty of French acting, as well as of English; and it was the more agreeable to him to converse with them upon these points in French—which language Mrs. Siddons, as well as John Kemble, spoke perfectly.

At last the evening was fixed for their public performance (at the theatre which was then close to the North Bridge, at the end of Prince's Street), and the moment it was announced as about to take place, every box and every available seat in the theatre was taken.

Lady Wemyss invited my father and mother to come to her box, but she neither asked her own daughter nor myself to do so, thinking perhaps that we were too young to enjoy such a privilege.

I felt dreadfully disappointed, but just at the eleventh hour good luck befell me; for my cousin, Mrs. Drummond Burrell, who was at that time staying at an hotel in St. Andrew's Square, had a box also; and upon her arrival at the theatre, she sent off Sir William Stuart, nephew of the late Sir William Drummond, of Logie Almond—so well known in the philosophical world—another cousin, to tell me to come to her immediately, as she had a place for me. Difficulties, however, still stood in the way, for the snow was thick on the ground. Sedan chairs were the fashion in Edinburgh, and at last one of these was found for me, but alas! with only one available porter, and wheels were useless on account of the snow. But my kind cousin, William Stuart, declared that he himself would act the part of the second porter, and so, with his help in carrying the chair, we at length started off.

As we entered the theatre the first piece was just beginning, and it was *The Gamester*, with Mrs. Siddons as the heroine. Previously, when I had met her at the house of Lady Drummond, I had thought her anything but young, and much too stout to be elegant, although nothing could deprive her of that inimitable grace, that easy *pose*, the idea of which is best portrayed in Sir Joshua Reynolds's celebrated picture of her as "The Tragic Muse."

But, when I saw her on the stage, I forgot her age, I forgot her size, I forgot even that the hero of the piece in which she was acting, was her own son, Henry Siddons. Spell-bound I watched her every movement, and the only thing real to me seemed the agonizing drama which was proceeding on the stage; and when at last, the Gamester was carried in apparently lifeless, and Mrs. Siddons, as Mrs. Beverley, in an attitude of terror, of which no words can convey an idea, fell down on her knees before him, then felt for the beating of his heart, and at last with one piercing shriek, exclaimed, "He is dead!" I screamed too.

Afterwards I saw Mrs. Siddons as Lady Macbeth. This part she of course acted splendidly, but it did not carry me away so much as her performance in *The Gamester* had done, for during it I did not, to the same extent, lose sight of her identity. As an illustration of my meaning, I may mention that when Mrs. Siddons, as Lady Macbeth, came on the stage in self-horror at the crime which had been perpetrated; and, looking—as though in the midst of some hideous dream—at her hands, said—"All the perfumes of Arabia cannot sweeten this little hand;" she then and there held up her hands, and they were not *little* hands at all, but very large ones, though well-shaped and white.

And yet the part of Lady Macbeth was that by which this great actress most wished to be remembered, as may be surmised from the following anecdote. One day, after Mrs. Siddons's retirement from the stage, a lady happened to call upon her, and found her pacing slowly up and down her garden, with an open book in her hand. The lady apologized for intruding on what evidently was a moment of anxious thought or study; but Mrs. Siddons, with a sort of sad smile, said, "No; you only find me with a book which, by this time, you would think I ought to know by heart; it is *Macbeth.* I thought that I did know my part in it well; but, alas! I have just now, *too late,* found out that I have *missed a point.*"

It was in the part of Coriolanus that I saw John Kemble at Edinburgh, and no words of mine can tell how the statuesque grandeur of his acting impressed me, combined as it was with certain heart-felt utterances (more especially when in dialogue with his mother), the tones of which made the hearer feel that, even in the case of this proud Roman, "one touch of nature maketh the whole world kin." Indeed, when witnessing John Kemble's acting I might well have forgotten what I now remember—that it was his niece who acted the part of his mother on that occasion. She was pretty, and acted her part charmingly. Surely it is the triumph of fine acting to make the audience forget the individuality of the actor, as was the case, more or less, with all the Kembles.

I am especially glad to remember Mrs. Siddons, as above stated, although my mother thought that I was still too young to go so much into society as I did at the date of my introduction to that "queen of tragedy." One thing, however, led to another, and after the theatrical excitement had a little subsided, that of balls began for me.

At that time—sixty years ago—the 18th of January was always celebrated in Edinburgh by an entertainment called the "Queen's Assembly." Lady Buchan was then the representative of Her Majesty, and of course nobody could be present at her assembly without a voucher, which was a sort of equivalent for a Lord Chamberlain's ticket at the Court balls in London.

Lord Buchan was one of my father's most intimate friends; and knowing the paternal indulgence exercised towards me, he asked me if I should like to accompany him to the ball. My answer may easily be surmised, and my father was only too willing to take me to the Assembly with him, although both my mother and Lady Buchan declared that I was much too young to be introduced there.

But in this case masculine prevailed over feminine influence, despite the French proverb, *Ce que Femme veut, le Ciel le veut.*

My mother did not enjoy general society equally with my father, but at home formed a *côterie* of her own, which resolved itself chiefly into daily, or rather evening, whist parties. Conspicuous at these were Lady Campbell (who lived at Holywood House), the old Duchesse de Grammont, a Portuguese lady who had married General Macdonald of Logary, and an old maid, Miss Grace Baillie. The latter, who still dressed quite youthfully, and was really popular in her way, was willing enough to play a rubber at whist as long as it did not cause her to miss a ball. And young people of both sexes in Edinburgh at that time were anxious for her presence at every festive gathering; for, unlike old maids generally, she was anxious to promote their enjoyment in every way, and her house was daily a pleasant afternoon rendezvous from two to five o'clock.

I do not know whether Miss Grace Baillie

voted either for or against my going to the "Queen's Assembly," but, despite the fact of my mother and Lady Buchan both protesting against my *entrée* there, and their united predictions that if I were "introduced" so early in life I should in a few years, and much to my own regret, be considered much older than my actual age, I did go. Lord Buchan assumed a sovereign will upon this point, and my father was delighted to introduce me at that, my first grand ball, to some of the Scottish beauties he had met a quarter of a century before at Drummond Castle. He had often spoken to me of these northern belles, but I, with the impertinence of extreme youth, had imagined that they long ago must have passed into the "sere and yellow leaf;" what, therefore, was my surprise when he presented me to two of them, and I found them both still beautiful! One of these ladies was Lady Charlotte Campbell (afterwards Lady Charlotte Bury), and the other was Miss Robertson, who lived to a great age, but died unmarried. The ball itself was brilliant. A famous musician of that day, named Niel Gow, was Strauss-like in his influence over the orchestra; but the beauty of the two ladies—my father's old friends—was the one thing chiefly remembered by me, and for years after that, my first evening at the "Queen's Assembly," they still remained celebrated for their personal charms.

In Edinburgh I often met Sir Walter Scott, and he taught me to play at chess. Never can I forget his kind but somewhat heavy-featured countenance, nor the sound of his friendly voice with its broad Scotch accent. He was frequently at the house of Miss Grace Baillie, and not only seemed pleased with the society of the many young persons he met there, but was always ready to enter into the spirit of any innocent jest that was going on amongst them. For example:—One day poor Miss Baillie having had one of her smart and too juvenile bead-embroidered dresses torn by some practical joke on the part of the mischievously merry Sir William Cumming Gordon, the latter promised her that he would import a lady's costume from France, which should surpass all dresses then in Edinburgh; on condition that, when it did arrive, it should be successively tried on by all the young ladies in the habit of frequenting Miss Grace Baillie's house. Sir William Cumming Gordon kept his promise, and in due course of time a packing-case arrived at Miss Baillie's. At its opening all her fair favourites were invited to be present, and not only these, but some gentlemen also, Sir Walter Scott among the number. The packing-case was opened, and many were the smiles of eager faces as from out of it was first lifted a blue cloth petticoat, all embroidered with gold; then a red jacket, also very grand; afterwards a costly lace neckerchief; then a wonderful Normandy cap, elaborately trimmed with lace to match the neckerchief, and last, not least, a pair of long earrings and large brooch, together with a magnificent cross to be worn round the neck.

It was a fancy-dress, but quite correct in all points of Normandy costume. Eagerly were the cap, the earrings, and the cross tried on by all the prettiest girls then in Edinburgh; but when at last it came to the turn of a Miss Mary Stuart to test their effect upon herself, she looked so extremely beautiful in them that Sir William Cumming Gordon fell down on his knees before her, and Sir Walter Scott, looking towards her at the same moment with amused admiration, repeated Pope's well-known lines—

> "On her white breast a sparkling cross she bore,
> That Jews might kiss and infidels adore."

Sir William Cumming Gordon, however, declared that though Jews might kiss the cross, he, as a Christian, would kiss the beautiful wearer of it. Here, however, propriety intervened, and he found himself suddenly prevented from fulfilling his Christian intentions.

Miss Baillie, who was at least fifty years old, and very tall and fat, had the good sense to know that this fancy dress was quite unsuited to herself, and she had also the good nature to form a raffle for it amongst her young friends about a week after its arrival from Paris.

She was certainly unwearied in her endeavours to promote amusement, and as the raffle was to take place at her own house, she made it the excuse for a fantastic fête, at which twelve little girls, dressed like shepherdesses, helped to conduct the numerous guests severally to their seats, before joining in the various Arcadian amusements provided for them. In a leafy bower sat a wizard fortune-teller, so disguised by his growth of venerable beard and imposing costume, that he was unrecognisable, although from his answers to those who came to hear their destinies from his lips, it was evident that he had had many social opportunities of studying the various characters of the company generally. Afterwards there was a ball, at which the lovely Miss Mary Stuart, who had drawn the prize at the raffle, wore the Normandy costume which so admirably became her.

CHAPTER IV.

SIR HENRY AND LADY M——Y—LORD AND LADY R——Y—MR. BEAUCLERC AND MISS B——R—LORD FIFE—MRS. STEIN—ST. BERNARD'S WELL—LADY AUGUSTA CLAVERING AND HER DAUGHTER—SIR WILLIAM CUMMING GORDON AND MISS BAILLIE—LORD BUCHAN—THE COMTE DE VALMONT—MISS WHARTON DUFF, ETC.—GRAND BALL ON BOARD SHIP.

CHAPTER IV.

IN Edinburgh before the Restoration, private theatricals, balls, card parties, and picnics fast succeeded each other. The gentlemen, many of them, drank deeply, but still their strong potations did not at other times prevent them from dancing and flirting. The social atmosphere was not, however, all cloudless, as will be seen by the two or three following anecdotes.

Sir Henry M——y and Lord R——y had, on the same day, married two sisters, who were both beautiful. These sisters strongly resembled each other in personal appearance, and the marriage of each of them was equally happy. But Lady M——y died in her first confinement, and Sir Henry was inconsolable. Lord and Lady R——y were unwearied in their attempts to soothe his grief, and in their society he for some time seemed more resigned than elsewhere, for he felt that they both sympathized in the cause of his anguish, and he knew that Lady R——y had been devotedly attached to her sister.

There was, nevertheless, anything but a permanent improvement in Sir Henry's state of mind, for, as months rolled on, his habitual gloom began to alternate so strangely with paroxysms of excitement, that my father, among others of the few old friends who could gain access to him in his dreary seclusion, began to fear for his reason. Lady R——y's sorrow, too, for her sister's loss seemed anything but ameliorated by time, although, unlike her widowed brother-in-law, she was constrained to appear occasionally in society with her husband. Well do I remember meeting her one day at a picnic; for young as I then was, and long since that time though it be, her grace and beauty combined with her air of melancholy in making an indelible impression upon me.

My father had known Lady R——y and her late sister in London, and had at one time continually met Sir Henry M——y at the house of his wife's father. He, therefore, on the day following that of the picnic, determined to go at once and pay his old acquaintance a visit.

Sir Henry M——y was at that time still staying with Lord and Lady R——y; and thither my father went. He found Sir Henry alone; but scarcely was he ushered into his presence when that grief-stricken man almost frantically exclaimed—"Take me away from this place; take me away. She puts me in mind of my lost wife, and I cannot bear it. Her look is the same; her manner is the same; her voice is so exactly like her sister's, that it actually makes me shudder. Sometimes I dread to go near her, and at other times I feel it impossible to exist a moment out of her sight. I really think I am out of my mind."

My father feared that insanity would indeed result from this state of agonized feeling, and he therefore lost no time in seeking Lord R——y, and declaring to him his conviction that an immediate change of scene was indispensable in the case of the unhappy man whom he had just left. Lord R——y coincided in this opinion, and at length, after further interviews, Sir Henry himself agreed to set forth on his travels in the course of a few days, every arrangement for his so doing having been in the meantime completed amongst his anxious friends.

But what took place in the course of those few days between Sir Henry M——y and Lady R——y none but themselves ever knew, for on the eve of the time fixed for his departure, she eloped with him, leaving her own husband, to whom she had hitherto seemed devoted, half mad himself with rage and despair. Whether or not pity was akin to love in this case, on the part of Lady R——y, who can say? Her flight caused more than a nine days' wonder at the time in Edinburgh, while the following circumstance, which happened not far from the same date, evoked more than nine days' indignation.

The Mr. Beauclerc before mentioned, having been introduced into the, at that period, somewhat exclusive social circle of the Modern Athens, by Lord Fife, was paying great attention to Miss B——r, a lady in age about thirty, and the independent possessor of some four thousand a year.

Her brother, who was in the army, was just

about this time ordered off to Madras with his regiment, and when he bade farewell to his sister, it was with the knowledge of her fast approaching marriage to Mr. Beauclerc. He feared that perhaps the large fortune of his sister might have had more than its due weight in Mr. Beauclerc's matrimonial choice, but he had no doubt whatever as to the good birth and position of his future brother-in-law.

The wedding dresses were all bought, the bridesmaids—six of them—were selected (myself one of them), and all Edinburgh began to talk of the marriage which was to take place in a month.

One day, just when matters and people were in this state of preparation and expectancy, I was with Miss B——r. Mr. Beauclerc was sitting by her side on a sofa, and we were all three talking as usual, when suddenly the door opened, and a Mr. Bruce, a friend of the brother of the bride-elect, was announced. He entered; but instead of advancing to pay his respects to Miss B——r, he stood mute with astonishment, while he gazed first at her and then at Mr. Beauclerc; until at last, addressing himself to the latter, he exclaimed,

"Why, Clark! what is the meaning of this?"

Mr. Beauclerc coloured, and seemed much confused, but he did not reply. Mr. Bruce then abruptly left the room; and half an hour afterwards a note was brought from him to Miss B——r, saying that of course he had no right to interfere in her affairs, but that still, as her brother's friend, he should like to know if she was aware that the pseudo Mr. Beauclerc was a billiard-marker known by the name of Clark in London.

In a sort of agony, Miss B——r read the note aloud, and then, passing it into the hand of her affianced husband, exclaimed, "Tell me, only tell me, that this is false!"

Pale as death, he looked at it, and forthwith rushed out of the room.

Miss B——r of course fainted, and the next day went into the country. But to continue, or rather to resume:—Conjecture was rife in Edinburgh as to the real cause of the charming Mr. Beauclerc's sudden disappearance; and there were some who, coupling it with Miss B——r's absence from that city, declared that he had run away with his intended wife.

Lord Fife, however, came back in course of time, and one evening, when Mr. Bruce met him at the house of Mrs. Stein, he entered into a long and serious explanation with his lordship as to the facts above recounted.

But, instead of looking as concerned as he ought to have done, considering that he was originally responsible for the introduction of the pseudo Mr. Beauclerc, Lord Fife burst out laughing, and exclaimed, "What a pity, Bruce, that you were, as you say, only just in time! What a pity! What a pity! Why, you know that he is really a most agreeable fellow, and money was all he wanted. Nay, he is so very superior to other billiard-markers, that in London he always goes by the name of the "Beau" Clark, and you yourself, Bruce, used to admire him and his curls very much. Poor fellow! I am very sorry for his disappointment—very sorry!"

The whole story then becoming generally known, everybody was very angry with Lord Fife—first, for having dared to introduce a billiard-marker, and then for only laughing at the consequences of such an introduction.

St. Bernard's Well had then a great reputation, not so much for its hygienic qualities as for its beautifying effects. No geologist had traced its hidden course, no physician of fame or fashion had published its virtues; but the flavour of its waters was like those of Harrogate; and as they had somehow gained a cosmetic reputation, St. Bernard's Well, or rather the picturesque locality in which it was situated, became a favourite scene for picnics. Chief amongst the leaders of these were the indomitable Miss Baillie and the frolicsome Sir William Cumming Gordon.

One belle of the company was a Miss Clavering, a brilliant brunette. Her general appearance left nothing to be desired; but, not content with being her own pretty self, she was always intent on personating the character of the heroine of the last novel she had happened to read. Sometimes, therefore, she was gay, and sometimes she was languishing, while various were the costumes worn by her as suitable to the several ideal beings she attempted successively, but not always successfully, to personate.

Her mother, Lady Augusta Clavering, was

her chaperon, and Sir William Cumming Gordon was one of her admirers.

Rambling about in different groups during an especial excursion to the Well, I remember the surprise of all, on one occasion, at the protracted absence of Miss Baillie. That genial old maid was nowhere to be seen; but some of us going back a little way, we espied her seated on a stile, and making frantic signals to us. Sir William Cumming Gordon had been apparently engrossed by his attentions to Lady Augusta Clavering and her daughter, and he declared that never before had he known Miss Clavering so fascinating; but, although hitherto attaching himself exclusively that morning to the fair Proteus and her mother, we found him running away in another direction, and laughing immoderately, as we approached the stile on which poor Miss Baillie was mysteriously perched, and in evident excitement. He had fled out of our sight. We thought his conduct eccentric, but it was not until we reached the stile that we became aware of the iniquitous cause of it. For there sat Miss Baillie immovable, but so inarticulate with rage that it was with some difficulty she explained to us how, just as she was about to get over the stile, Sir William had, with a great show of politeness, presented himself to assist her in that awkward operation; and how, entirely trusting to his aid, she had put one foot over the top-bar, and was carefully drawing her dress after her, when, quick as lightning, he knotted her ankles together with a pocket-handkerchief, and ran off as fast as his legs could carry him. Of course we all shared Miss Baillie's indignation, and lost no time in extricating her, while the delinquent had meanwhile rejoined Lady Augusta Clavering and her daughter, and was helping them over the stepping-stones of a brook with the utmost politeness.

Afterwards, when Lady Augusta was made aware of the trick that had been practised upon poor Miss Baillie, she joined her entreaties with those of the rest of the company in persuading that discomfited lady to accept Sir William's profuse apologies; but this not until he had bound himself to take twenty numbers for a raffle that was about to be held under the offended lady's superintendence.

Peace being thus restored, we that day went, as had been settled, to the house of Mr. James Erskine, who resided in the neighbourhood, and there we found my father and his friend, Lord Buchan, awaiting us. And here I cannot glance back at the luncheon that followed, during which even the still lingering cloud on Miss Baillie's brow gradually cleared off, without recalling one or two of the many points of the conversation by which Lord Buchan was generally wont to amuse people. Lord Buchan was, to all appearance, scarcely sixty years of age; but upon that day he protested that he was at least a hundred. "For," said he, in explanation of this paradox, "I never sleep more than five hours, and I have never had an hour's illness; and when I calculate the time most people sleep beyond five hours, and then add to it the time usually taken up each year by illness, I find that the balance is so much on my side that I am, at least, a centenarian."

Lord Buchan was a Protestant, but, nevertheless, he believed in the miraculous power of faith, as proved by the following anecdote.

The Comte de Valmont was at one time

staying with him at Kirkhill, Linlithgowshire, where stood a small Roman Catholic chapel in ruins. He was taken dangerously ill during this visit with typhus fever; and though the most eminent physicians were summoned to his aid, the malady was of such a fearful character that in a short time no expectation whatever was entertained of his recovery. Lord Buchan was told that his young friend's case was utterly hopeless, and it was then that he caused the Comte, who was quite insensible, to be carried on a mattress into the ruined chapel. Six men transported him thither, and deposited him not far from the altar, on which lay a small phial of holy oil. The altar was in a better state of preservation than the rest of the chapel, which had not been used since the Revolution. When Lord Buchan was left with the dying man and one of the physicians, he reverently took the phial, opened it, and after praying earnestly, moistened his finger with the holy oil, and making the sign of the cross, anointed his unconscious friend, adhering as closely as possible to the ceremonial he knew to be customary with those of the creed of the Comte de Valmont, who was a Roman Catholic.

The physician in attendance watched Lord Buchan's proceeding, but he had no faith in it whatever, and was only sorry to perceive that his lordship cherished some absurd expectation of benefit to be derived from it. What, therefore, was the surprise of this disciple of Æsculapius when, after his dying patient was carried back to his bed in a still insensible condition, he beheld him open his eyes, while a gleam of life passed over his countenance! The doctor at once administered a powerful stimulant, and from that moment the young Comte gradually revived; and at length his most unexpected recovery was pronounce complete. The physician afterwards maintained that the fresh air inhaled by his patient in, and on his way to, the ruined chapel, had so far restored his feeble vitality as to enable the medicine subsequently given to him to take effect; but Lord Buchan always declared that the recovery was a miracle.

Sometimes, during that time in Scotland, we made excursions along the shore in small sailing boats. The party on these occasions was usually composed of Lady Campbell and her daughter, the Misses Davison, Mr. Bruce, Lord Fingall, Lady Harriet Plunkett and her brother, Mr. Buller, Miss Wharton Duff, my father, and myself. Miss Wharton Duff's vivacity was excessive. Mr. Buller was much attached to her; but her restless nature and her recklessness of danger often placed him, as her true and trusty knight, in somewhat ludicrous positions. For example, one day, when the gentlemen of our excursion party had stayed to fish, Miss Wharton Duff amused herself by climbing up alone to the top of an immense rock, and soon growing tired of admiring the splendid view visible from her solitary situation, she essayed a descent from it; but in this case it was more difficult to come down than to mount. Presently, therefore, when we looked up, we were horrified to behold Miss Wharton Duff hanging on painfully by her hands to a slab of the rock, with nothing whatever beneath upon which to place her feet. Her position was so imminently dangerous that we shuddered lest in a moment she might be dashed to pieces; and Mr. Buller, terrified at what seemed her impending fall, flew to her assistance at great risk to himself. In his desperate efforts to reach her, he stumbled again and again over the large masses of broken and rugged rock that lay in his way; but what was his astonishment when, at last within ear-shot of her, he heard her greet every fresh fall of his with a peal of laughter!

He rescued her, but at the cost of such injury to himself that, having deposited her in safety, he was conveyed to a cottage near, and there he lay for more than three weeks afterwards in a state of much suffering from his bruises. Miss Wharton Duff laughed on still; in fact, everything seemed to be a cause of merriment to her; but when Mr. Buller reappeared, it only too soon became evident to her that his admiration of her had considerably cooled since the adventure so well nigh fatal to both their lives.

Miss Wharton Duff still continued to laugh in company, but she keenly felt Mr. Buller's neglect, for she preferred him to everybody else; and it was therefore with a heavy heart that she still kept up the appearance of a smiling countenance until the time when a splendid ball was given by Sir Francis Sykes (at that time Captain Sykes) on board his ship, then lying off Leith.

This ship could not be brought nearer than two miles to shore, and the intermediate distance had, therefore, to be traversed in small boats. Miss Wharton Duff (like all the other members of our own immediate circle) was to be present at this ball; and indeed all the arrangements made on board ship for the entertainment were magnificent. On arriving at the vessel's side, a throne-like chair was lowered, in which the ladies were successively lifted on deck without any injury to their dresses. Bouquets and tablets for the dancers were then presented to each of them by the ship's officers, and so minute in detail had been the gallantry of these gentlemen in preparing for our reception, that in a cabin, fitted up as a dressing-room or boudoir, we found various female attendants awaiting us; and under their superintendence stood tables piled up with gloves, fans, scents, shoes, and many other such appurtenances of a lady's toilette, not even needles and thread being forgotten. The quarter and main decks were covered in, and these, with the saloon, formed four large compartments, which were hung with a variety of flags—some of them war trophies—rich tapestry, and scarfs of foreign texture and dazzling hues, all shining with gold and silver embroidery.

The music was inspiring, for not only was the ship's band in high practice for the occasion, but the then celebrated Niel Gow was pressed into the orchestral service. Dancing began, and everybody was gay, except that generally merriest of merry persons, Miss Wharton Duff, for she was suffering tortures from a violent toothache. Whether the sense of Mr. Buller's coldness towards her made it worse, I cannot say; but at length the pain became so unbearable that she determined then and there to have the offending tooth extracted by the ship-surgeon. He was summoned, and she went through the operation with the greatest fortitude, and after it was over she joined the dancers, restored to her usual gaiety. The sudden relief from acute physical pain was evident in this agreeable change, but, as after-events indicated, it was probably inspired also by the equally sudden return of hope to her heart. She danced several times with Mr. Buller, growing on each occasion more and more animated, until she became more charming than she had ever appeared before. When the hour of departure came, he carefully wrapped her cloak around her so as to protect her from cold, and then descended after her into the boat that was about to convey her and others from the ship to the shore.

Within a short date from that night of the ball they were married. Forty years afterwards I met them both at Brighton, and their happiness seemed none the less complete. She was wayward as of old, but he rejoiced in humouring all her whims as though she still were young and beautiful.

CHAPTER V.

DEPARTURE FROM HOLYROOD—LONDON—THE PRINCE REGENT—THE DUCHESSE D'ANGOULEME—THE COMTE D'ARTOIS AND THE DUC DE BERRY—THE EMPEROR OF RUSSIA AND THE KING OF PRUSSIA—THE EMPRESS JOSEPHINE—ALMACK'S—BALLET IN LONDON—LORD BYRON—GRAND CALEDONIAN BALL—THE DUC AND DUCHESSE D'ORLEANS—THE ROULETTE TABLE IN PARIS—TALLEYRAND—COUNT D'ORSAY—SINGULAR PREDICTION AND ITS FULFILMENT—THE BROTHERS POLIGNAC.

CHAPTER V.

THE time of the Restoration was at hand. The Comte d'Artois had already left Holyrood House, and my father made arrangements to follow quickly in his footsteps. My grandmother, the Duchess of Melfort, was at that time eighty-eight years of age, but like my mother, Lady Maurice Drummond, she joyfully anticipated a speedy return to France in the train of the long exiled Bourbons. It was decided that at first we should go by sea to London, there to await political events. With our family party travelled Lady Campbell, her son and daughter, the Comte de Coigny, the Chevalier de Rebourguille, and the Comte de Béranger, a nephew of my grandmother.

We were eight days in achieving the voyage from Leith Harbour to London, but the journey by no means wearied us, for the vessel was well fitted up, and we (the younger travellers) danced every evening; while my father and mother, with the Comte de Coigny and the Chevalier de Rebourguille played at whist. Once, certainly, there was a break in these amusements, for during a dense fog the vessel ran upon a sand-bank. This danger, however, was of no long duration, and we were all in high spirits when at last we arrived at Blackwall. There we agreed that each person of our party should name two dishes, and our united selection produced a dinner not unworthy of Brillat Savarin himself. After partaking of this, we all set off that same evening for London. The metropolis was at that time very gay, for all classes of people, from the Prince Regent downwards, seemed to rejoice in the restoration of the Bourbons. White flags were flying in honour of them, and white cockades were in fashion. The Prince Regent had himself gone down as far as Stanmore to offer his congratulations to Louis XVIII when that long banished monarch was on his way from Hartwell (the English abode of his exile) to London; and in the capital itself, everybody was eager to gain a glimpse of the

King of France, and still more so of his companion and niece, his *Antigone*, as he called her—the Duchesse d'Angoulême, daughter of the martyred Louis XVI. and Marie Antoinette, and the sharer in her youth of their captivity, generally known to Europe as the "Orphan of the Temple."

Congratulatory addresses were on every side offered to Louis XVIII., whose advent in France was heralded under the *sobriquet* of "The Father of his People." The elder of the two surviving brothers of "Louis the Martyr" was not a hero in appearance, and, therefore, legitimists in France, where tradition still clung to the warlike deeds of Bourbons in bygone times, felt it expedient to prepare the minds of the people for the sight of a King whose infirm legs were cased in red velvet gaiters, whose body, no longer slender, was buttoned up in a blue surtout, and who wore on his head a round English hat. So Louis XVIII. was proclaimed beforehand as the father of his people and as "the Magistrate King," who was coming to give France peace, now that the sanguinary despotism of Napoleon was over, and to grant her a Constitution instead of the fancied glory which had cost her so much blood and treasure.

Accompanied by the Prince Regent, Louis XVIII. and the Duchesse d'Angoulême reached Dover. The Comte d'Artois, with his two sons, the Duc d'Angoulême and the Duc de Berry, had preceded His Majesty to Paris, and thither we, like other legitimists, were to follow them immediately; but London at that moment was very attractive. There I saw for the first time the Emperor Alexander and the King of Prussia. The former was a remarkably handsome man, both in face and figure, and in the eyes of my family he was invested with a peculiar interest on account of his generous conduct towards the Empress Joséphine, who, when Vicomtesse de Beauharnais, was much beloved by many of my relatives.

In London, in 1814, Mrs. Drummond Burrell (afterwards Lady Willoughby d'Eresby) was occasionally my chaperon. She was one of the Lady Patronesses of Almack's.

At Almack's, in 1814, Scotch reels and the country-dances of Old England were still in fashion, though the quadrille and valse were then recently introduced. The conventions decreed by the Ladies Patronesses were so strictly adhered to, that one night when the Duke of Wellington arrived a few minutes after twelve, the hour after which it had been decided no visitor should be admitted, he was refused admission to the ball-room.

In the same year I first went to the opera in London. A ballet was performed, but the style of dancing in it was quite different from that in the present day; for it was easy and graceful, but so little exaggerated that it would have offered no very extraordinary spectacle in a drawing-room; and the dresses worn by the "ladies of the ballet" were nearly down to their ankles. I first met Lord Byron at that time in London, and his appearance made a melancholy impression on me. He was extremely handsome, and was much courted by everybody; but his manner, when in general society, was so shy and retiring that he would hardly ever move from the side of the room where he had happened to take a position on his first entrance into it. This peculiarity was, I believe, attributable to his lameness, a defect of which he was ever painfully conscious, and the sense of which no doubt enhanced the air of sadness that generally pervaded his look and manner.

He was an object of general attention among ladies, even before the time when Lady Caroline Lamb is said to have poisoned herself, stabbed herself, and drowned herself—unsuccessfully—for his sake. Beautiful women of rank vied with each other in a manifest wish to attract the notice of the poet. They learned his verses by heart, but it is strange that but few, if any, of them had intelligence or individuality enough to attire herself according to a poet's fancy; for anything rather than ideal was the mode of English ladies' dress in those days, especially when it was surmounted, as usual then on grand occasions at Court, by three large white feathers—a "Prince of Wales's plume"—which rose above the head of the fair wearer to the height of at least half a yard. No wonder that George III., beholding these plumes waving before him when he opened Parliament just at the time when his reason began to totter, addressed himself to "My Lords and Peacocks!"

My grandmother, the Duchess of Melfort, presented a rather singular but by no means unpicturesque appearance in those days of her sojourn in London, before her return to France. She was, as I have said, at that time eighty-eight years of age; she had lived to see many strange fashions of all sorts succeed each other, but that of her own dress was still of the time of Louis XV. She was in full possession of all her faculties, and so unimpaired was her bodily strength that one of her favourite amusements was to walk with my brother, who was then only seven years old, and Madame d'Aubigny, who had never been in London before, to Kensington Palace, which was then quite out of town. She delighted in the beautiful gardens which extended at that time round the palace, and especially rejoiced in wandering through a maze-like plantation of shrub-lilacs which helped to adorn them. Here, where she had sometimes a difficulty in threading her way through the labyrinth, the Duke of Kent often met her. Her conversation was rich with the stores of long experience, or, at all events, His Royal Highness seemed to find it so; for after helping her to find her way through the lilac bushes, he was in the frequent habit of walking home with her, chatting all the way; and after each of these interviews he would call the next day to inquire how she felt after her long walk. I need not add that my grandmother was pleased with this attention, and was wont, while smoothing down the soft satin folds of her Louis Quinze blue robe, to declare that the Duke of Kent was the most charming and well-bred man she had ever met.

Balls and parties rapidly succeeded each other during our short stay in London, for all the embassies vied with each other in the splendour of their several fêtes to celebrate the Restoration; but by many foreigners of distinction at that time in England the Caledonian Ball was considered the most remarkable. The Highland costume worn upon this occasion by all Scotch gentlemen present, was strange to continental eyes. Each chieftain wore his own tartan, and the combination of colours was dazzling. More amazing still to the uninitiated were the Scottish country dances, and particularly the reel, with its rapid steps, its Highland fling, and the wild yell of triumph, like that of the Red Indian, shouted forth by its dancers.

At that ball all Scotch ladies likewise wore their national costume according to clan; and my cousin, Mrs. Drummond Burrell, wore the Drummond tartan dress, trimmed with gold fringe; while I, who accompanied her, felt by no means displeased at myself, arrayed as I was in white, trimmed with Drummond tartan, shoes to match, and a scarf of the same plaid fastened with a large brooch on the left shoulder.

It was not long, however, before, by going from London to Paris, we exchanged one scene of gaiety for another; and to me Paris at that period was like fairyland. Louis XVIII. was installed at the Tuileries by the time we reached the capital from which he had been so long exiled, and the Duc and Duchesse d'Orléans were at the Palais Royal. The Duc d'Orléans (afterwards Louis Philippe, King of the French) had shown great fortitude during the years of adversity which had intervened between the time of the Revolution of 1793, when, as a mere youth, he had been constrained to fly from France, and that when, as a husband and a father, he returned to the Palais Royal, the scene of his childhood. His father (Egalité) had perished on the scaffold, but his mother, the dowager Duchesse d'Orléans, was still alive to participate in memories so overwhelming, that under their influence he (the future Citizen King of the French) with the greatest difficulty prostrated himself and kissed the marble pavement of the Palais Royal when he again first crossed its threshold after the Restoration.

His wife, Marie Amélie, Duchesse d'Orléans, was from the first an object of much interest to the people of Paris, not only on account of the many virtues she possessed, but because she was a niece of Marie Antoinette, and daughter of Queen Caroline of Naples, who had done so much politically to avenge the martyrdom of her royal sister.

Presently we shall enter more fully into the inner circle of Court life in France during the reign of Louis XVIII.; but previous to my own presentation at the Tuileries, I saw enough of Paris society to delight me, though some few points in it struck me as very peculiar. For example, at some of the best frequented soirées a well-known Marquis d'Ivry presided at a roulette table, having been appointed by Government to do so; and Prince Talleyrand, my father's old friend, would sit at this table, putting on it handful after handful of gold and notes, but never showing, by the slightest change of countenance, whether he was winning or losing. Many ladies of rank also gambled at this roulette table (which used to be conveyed by its owner from house to house), and amongst these ladies I especially remember the Comtesse d'Arquito, a beautiful Italian about thirty years of age. Dancing was often going on in rooms contiguous to that set apart for gambling, but such terrible fascination had the roulette table for the lady above named, that she could not be induced to leave it for a moment in favour of any other amusement. At the house of General Bradshaw the roulette table would make its appearance, but balls were especially brilliant there, and it was at one of them that I first met Count d'Orsay. He was then only nineteen years of age, and was still the "Jeune Cupidon," as Byron called him. His father, who before the Revolution had been known as "le beau d'Orsay," was still very handsome, though quite in a different style from his son; and Count d'Orsay's sister, the Duchesse de Grammont, was one of the most lovely women I ever saw, and very like her father.

At the time of the Restoration the Emperor Alexander was everywhere most welcome. Talleyrand gladly received him under his own roof, and was therefore said to have made him his prisoner.

Speaking of the Emperor Alexander, I must once more here connect his name with that of Joséphine, who, with her daughter Hortense, owed much to his generosity. He was the last guest entertained, and this only on the eve of her death, by the ex-Empress.

I myself saw Joséphine two years before the time when she unexpectedly breathed the last sigh of her troubled and eventful life. She was then at Malmaison, whither I was taken by my father. Though no longer young, she was still pre-eminently graceful, and her pliant though not tall figure showed to advantage in a white dress, magnificently embroidered in bright colours that assorted well with her dark hair, worn low on the forehead, and with the fine eyes of deep violet hue, by which her expressive face was illumined.

I remember, too, the room in which I saw her. It was hung with crimson cloth and gold, and every fauteuil and sofa in it was ornamented with large ivory balls—a very effective style of ornament, and one which struck me very much.

Joséphine loved Napoleon better than she loved herself. Childless by her marriage with him (though the mother of a son and daughter by her first less happy union with the Vicomte de Beauharnais), she voluntarily consented to her divorce from him for the sake of the perpetuation of his dynasty. She had survived that dishonour, if so it may be called, in her own life; she had descended the steps of the throne on which the Emperor had seated her beside him; but she could not survive his downfall, and she died when sentence of exile to Elba was passed upon him.

My readers may remember how Cagliostro had predicted to Joséphine, when she went to him in company with my grandmother, that she would be "more than Queen of France," and yet that she would "die on a dunghill."

My grandmother was much struck by the truth of this prediction, when the time of its fulfilment came; but in explanation of it I may again mention that Malmaison, the last home and deathbed scene of Joséphine, had been in times previous to her tenure of the property, a place upon which heaps of common refuse were allowed to be flung—in fact, a *fumier*, or dunghill, to the stables.

It was difficult to remember this fact when beholding Malmaison, as I did, a lovely Château surrounded by beautiful gardens, odoriferous with those rare flowers which the ex-Empress loved to cultivate, and replete with every ornament that her fine taste could lavish upon it.

One room at Malmaison was especially consecrated by Joséphine to the memories of happy days passed there by Napoleon in the time before his divorce from her. It was a room then used by him as a study, whenever the cares of war and politics permitted him to seek a temporary rest in her society in that charming retreat; and when she was left there alone to mourn their separation, she would allow nobody to occupy this room but herself. In it lay the pen last used there by the Emperor, which the ink had long since corroded; on a table lay the map he had last studied there, the line of march tracked out in which had long since taught Europe to feel the power of his tactics; and on the wall hung a glass case in which some of his hair was arranged in ornamental or symbolic form. It was so long since that hair had grown on his head, that the sight of it must have carried back Joséphine's memory to the time when she, the widowed Vicomtesse de Beauharnais, determined on marrying its owner, the young soldier of fortune, with nothing but "his love, and his sword, and his cloak to offer her." Such a sanctuary indeed was this chamber at Malmaison to the ex-Empress, that she would not allow any hand but her own to dust or move the objects in it, which had been consecrated, as she deemed, by the touch of the husband who had sacrificed her to his ambition, and in so doing had lost the guiding star, the guardian angel, of his life.

One bad effect to Napoleon of his divorce

from Joséphine, was the offence given by that act to the clergy and the *ancien régime*, to which she belonged, both in right of her birth and by her first marriage, and the members of which it was his wisest policy to conciliate. It was by her influence that, after his first installation at the Tuileries, many of the most powerful families by inheritance in France lent him their countenance, if not their active support; and indeed Joséphine herself, though the devoted wife of Napoleon, had such vivid memories of the Court of Marie Antoinette, and such a remembrance of that ill-fated Queen, to whom she had been personally attached, that it was with pain rather than with pride she found herself reigning in her stead at the Tuileries, at St. Cloud, at Fontainebleau, and elsewhere.

The attachment of Joséphine to the class from which she herself had originally sprung, and to which her son and daughter, Eugène and Hortense, belonged by inheritance, is generally well known; but not so the following anecdote, which I owe to my grandmother, the Duchess of Melfort.

The Polignac family was high in Court favour in the old days before the Revolution, and Joséphine, then Vicomtesse de Beauharnais, was necessarily well acquainted with the Princesse de Polignac, the favourite friend of the Queen, and the governess of Her Majesty's children. It will therefore be easily understood that when the two brothers Polignac (in the confidence of the exiled Comte d'Artois) were declared by Fouché's spies to have conspired in the Pichegru plot in 1803-4 against Bonaparte's life, Joséphine did all she could to shield them from the emissaries of the police; and this she achieved with such success that, when the elder Polignac was condemned to death, and his brother, Jules, to imprisonment, they neither of them were anywhere to be found.

My grandmother was then still resident at the Château de St. Germain, and she being in the confidence of Joséphine, it was there that the elder Polignac was concealed while the government agents were elsewhere vainly searching for him far and near.

Jules de Polignac, the younger brother, though also out of reach of detection, wrote a letter to Bonaparte, confessing that he, in some sort, had been concerned in the conspiracy, but using this confession as an appeal to the First Consul's clemency in behalf of his elder brother, who, unlike himself, was married and had a large family. But the confession and appeal were alike in vain, and, there seemed no hope of pardon for either of them.

One day when Bonaparte was particularly elated with some stroke of military success, Joséphine approached him, and said—"I am distressed beyond measure to hear of the frightful sentence passed against the Polignacs—they were always my friends—do you think either sentence just? What proof have you of their guilt?"

"Most undeniable proof," answered Bonaparte. And he showed her the letter which Jules de Polignac had written to him. She took it into her hand, and quietly asked—"Is this the only proof you have of their guilt?"

"Yes," answered he, "and quite enough." But the words had scarcely left his mouth ere, looking round, he saw Jules de Polignac's letter flaming in the fire.

Bonaparte was angry, but Joséphine was

still at that time the idol of his life, and he forgave her, saying that, though she had destroyed the letter, the fact of its contents was patent to others besides himself.

Time went on; the terrible fate of the Duc d'Enghien had struck grief into the hearts of those who were nearest and dearest to Bonaparte, and he himself had received a violent shock by Pichegru's suicide in prison. But where were the Polignacs? De Rivière, one of the conspirators, had been pardoned, partly, as Bonaparte himself afterwards said, "by the prayers of Murat;" and Joséphine thought that she might now at length act in favour of the brothers who already owed their safety to her. One day, therefore, on arriving at St. Cloud, the first Consul became conscious of some sort of extraordinary excitement going on in his wife's apartments there; and to Count Lavalette, who was in attendance upon him, expressed curiosity as to the cause of it. Bonaparte himself was much agitated that day; he seemed distressed to have found Joséphine in tears; and whilst he walked up and down his cabinet, murmured,—"The wretches wanted to murder me. What a base act!" "A little while afterwards," explains Count Lavalette, "he encountered M. de Rivière and the female relations of the Polignacs, led on by Joséphine, who fell at his feet; and it must have been then that, as afterwards recounted by my grandmother, he saw before him two figures, draped from head to foot in white. Were they statues, or were they human beings travestied for some cunning tableau-vivant?

Joséphine looked up to Bonaparte, and said to him—"Your power is unlimited; no wonder that you are victorious! Look, now, at those two silent figures, they are as still as death; but you have only to say, 'Live!' and forthwith they will awaken to life."

Bonaparte smiled sadly, but she, persisting still, continued, "Nay, to please *me*, do but say the word, 'Live!'"

Then, falling into her humour, he called out aloud, "Live!"

And the two statuesque figures suddenly came forward and fell on their knees at his feet. It is needless to add that they were the two brothers Polignac, and that it was thus they owed their lives to Joséphine.

CHAPTER VI.

PRESENTATION AT THE TUILERIES TO LOUIS XVIII. AND THE DUCHESSE D'ANGOULEME—PAST LIFE OF THE DUCHESSE D'ANGOULEME—THE DUCHESSE D'ORLEANS (AFTERWARDS QUEEN OF THE FRENCH)—SOCIAL RELATIONS BETWEEN THE TUILERIES AND THE PALAIS ROYAL—DAILY DOMESTIC LIFE AT THE TUILERIES—MADAME LA COMTESSE DE CAYLA—VISIT OF LOUIS XVIII TO VERSAILLES AND TRIANON.

CHAPTER VI.

NOT long after our arrival in Paris, I was presented to Louis XVIII. and his niece, the Duchesse d'Angoulême, by Lady Stuart, the English Ambassadress. Nobody could at that time behold the Duchesse d'Angoulême doing the honours of the Tuileries without a feeling of pathetic interest, and least so those who, like many surviving relatives of mine, could remember her in her early youth, before the fatal storming of the Tuileries caused her, then only upon the threshold of womanhood, to exchange a palace for a prison. Upon the 10th of August, 1792, she had fled with her parents, Louis XVI. and Marie Antoinette, from the palace of the Tuileries, then in the power of the insurgent mob, and eventually found herself a captive in the prison of the Temple. During the first days of her detention there she still enjoyed the company of her august parents, of her saint-like aunt, the Princesse Elisabeth, and of her brother, the Dauphin. Various attendants, including the lovely and devoted Princesse de Lamballe, formed a suite to the unfortunate Royal Family, but this for a very short time only. Gradually these faithful followers were torn away from the side of the King and Queen, to whose adverse fortunes they had clung, and at last even Louis XVI. and Marie Antoinette were separated in that dreary prison of the Temple from each other's society.

The Duchesse d'Angoulême, called from her cradle by right of birth, Madame Royale of France, fainted at the feet of her father on the eve of his execution, for she dearly loved him. After his martyrdom was accomplished, she did all that lay in her power to comfort her widowed mother, until the removal of the latter from the prison of the Temple to the dungeon of the Conciergerie, separated them for ever in this world. Not certain of her mother's death, but fearing the worst, she then found herself left in the prison of the Temple, bereft even of the necessaries of life.

Her aunt, the pious Madame Elisabeth, was at that time her only companion, for her brother, the Dauphin (or, rather, Louis XVII., since his father's execution) had some time before been taken from her by the infamous cruelty which terminated in his death. At last, however, she found herself absolutely alone in her prison, for her aunt was also led forth from it to the guillotine.

For nineteen months after that last separation the condition of the princess was that of solitary confinement, of absolute isolation, in that terrible prison of the Temple. She knew that the crime of regicide had been accomplished in the case of her father, but she was still in a state of agonized suspense as to the fate of her mother, her aunt, and her brother. She was then scarcely sixteen years of age, but she strove to bear the unprecedented misery of her position with resignation. In the depth of winter, and alone in the chill gloom of her cell, she may have remembered the brightness of Versailles in her childhood; she may have remembered beloved and sunlit countenances there;

she had no face in prison to smile upon her, but she may have remembered also how her father had bidden her, at her first communion, hold fast her faith in adversity. To this faith she clung, while, still a solitary captive, months succeeded months, mostly drearily to her. Through her barred windows she observed the days grow shorter and shorter, or longer and longer, and at last, by counting them, she knew that her winter birthday (it was in December) had come round again, and that she was seventeen years of age.

But that was the day of her deliverance from the prison of the Temple. Robespierre was dead; the Reign of Terror was over; and she was to be sent forthwith (in an exchange of prisoners) to Vienna, there to claim a shelter from her maternal kinsfolk, though in point of fact they were absolute strangers to her.

She was scarcely more than a child when she entered the prison of the Temple, but she was a woman, a sorrowful woman, when she left it. After nineteen months of absolute isolation from her fellow-creatures, she was set at liberty. But what charm had liberty now to her? For alas! she had been told at last that all those who had made life dear to her were dead.

In early childhood, however, she had been betrothed to her cousin, the Duc d'Angoulême, eldest son of the Comte d'Artois, afterwards Charles X. Many years had elapsed since she had seen or heard of the boy-bridegroom who at one time used to play with her at the Little Trianon, or by whose side she was made to stand during some grand Court ceremonial at Versailles. Her memory of him had grown faint, but not so that of the wish of her parents that she should be his wife.

When, therefore, she met him at last again, after a brief sojourn at Vienna, and at Mittau, she married him in the presence of her uncle, Louis XVIII., then resident in exile there, and of numerous royalists who had flocked from their scattered homes out of France far and near, to witness the celebration of an event which they hoped would perpetuate the Royal dynasty of France.

But the Duc and Duchesse d'Angoulême were childless. For years subsequent to her not too happy marriage the Duchesse had been the devoted companion of her uncle, Louis XVIII., at Hartwell, near Aylesbury. After the Restoration it was with strangely mingled feelings that the Princess found herself again—she being then much more than thirty years of age—in the scenes of her youth. So overpowering indeed were her emotions on returning to Paris after so many years' absence, that when the carriage which conveyed her turned towards the Tuileries by the Pont Neuf, she fainted, as she had fainted at her father's feet in prison on the night before his execution. It was by the side of Louis XVIII. that she made her entry into Paris, and some among the crowd were inclined to resent the tears flowing from her eyes on an occasion of so much public rejoicing in honour of her family; but when the people beheld her conveyed towards the palace of her ancestors pale and motionless, like one already dead, every heart for the moment was moved with compassion.

The old nobility of France soon crowded to the Tuileries for presentation to the Princess, but at first she only received a dozen persons at a time. Upon these occasions the ladies were all dressed in white, and wore coronets of *Fleur de Lys.*

The resemblance of Madame Royale, Duchesse d'Angoulême, to her mother, Marie Antoinette, was then generally observed; but it was the resemblance of cold marble to animated flesh and blood. I was still very young when I was presented to this Princess, and perhaps I did not make sufficient allowance for the fact that she had been too long schooled by the world's cruel coldness to herself and those whom in early youth she had loved best, to permit herself much outward demonstration of kindly emotion. Upon great occasions the Duchesse d'Angoulême rose supreme, but the general tenor of her life was more fit for a cloister than a palace.

Thus it came to pass that, before the arrival of the Duchesse de Berry as bride to the younger brother of the Duc d'Angoulême, the entertainments at the Tuileries were by no means so brilliant as elsewhere in Paris. The receptions at the Palais Royal were far more popular. The Duchesse d'Angoulême politically distrusted the Duc d'Orléans (afterwards

King Louis Philippe), the host of the Palais Royal, and did not always care to conceal her dislike of him; but she was extremely friendly to his consort (afterwards Queen Marie Amélie) between whom and herself there were some points of resemblance. The Duchesse d'Orléans, though by birth a Neapolitan Princess, was remarkably quiet and grave in her demeanour, and looking first at her as the daughter of the ambitious and restless Queen Caroline of Naples, and then at her cousin the Duchesse d'Angoulême, the daughter of the brilliant and fascinating Queen Marie Antoinette, it was surprising how unlike in manner these princesses, the offspring of sister Queens, were to both of them, though, perhaps, in seriousness of character they both resembled their late grandmother, Maria Theresa, the great Empress-Queen of Austria and Hungary.

Upon the return of Louis XVIII. to the Tuileries various attempts were made to revive the etiquette, and even the costume, of the Court of France before the Revolution; but the precarious health of the King on the one hand, and the retired habits of the Duchesse d'Angoulême on the other, forbade the frequency of brilliant entertainments, such as those which, it will be remembered, were inaugurated after the arrival of the Duchesse de Berry.

Ordinarily the King dined with the Royal Family between five and six o'clock. On these occasions His Majesty only was seated in an arm-chair. His brother—Monsieur—the Comte d'Artois, and his two sons, the Ducs d'Angoulême and de Berry, occupied seats without arms, as did also the Duchesse d'Angoulême. Conversation was animated enough at these daily dinners of the Royal Family at the Tuileries, and the Princes, when at table, were in the habit of now and then addressing the officers of their several households in attendance upon them.

After dinner the Comte d'Artois usually adjourned to the pavilion, or part of the palace assigned to him; and while the Duc and Duchesse d'Angoulême enjoyed his society, or the privacy of their own domestic life, the King amused himself with the chatty companionship of the Comtesse de Cayla, his favourite, who tells us that, worn out with the duties and the occupations of the day (to say nothing of the physical infirmities to which the Duchesse d'Angoulême had ministered with the patience of a Sister of Charity in an hospital), His Majesty was then in need of distraction, and called the time of her being with him *les heures de délassement royal.* Then she declares began a *causerie gaie et piquante.* The anecdotes of the day were passed in review. Madame de Cayla did not reside at the Tuileries, but at her own hotel in the vicinity. The anecdotes of the day at the Tuileries were therefore not generally known to her until the evening.

The King one day had been to Versailles, the place of his birth, and where all his youth had been passed. Paris was full of the works of Napoleon; the Louvre, the Tuileries, the Place du Carrousel, the Quais, a whole crowd of buildings, all recalled to his mind the reign of Bonaparte. It was not so at Versailles. That palace, that park, those solitary groves, were still eloquent of the *grand siècle;* for he who had scattered his trophies all over France, who had continued the Louvre, who had draped Notre Dame with banners, emblematic of his victories, had not considered himself rich enough to refurnish and restore Versailles, with due regard to the *prestige* appertaining to that former abode of the Grand Monarque.

"It was a pleasure to breathe," said Louis XVIII. to the Comtesse de Cayla, "in that cherished abode of my ancestors: its pompous solitude charmed me even more than my reception at the Tuileries had done. I liked to wander through those walks, those flower-gardens, and, above all, through those immense halls and that vast gallery, where everything transported me back to another time. I entered the apartments I once inhabited there, and when I reached my former study I requested to be left alone there for an instant. A few pieces of furniture had been hastily placed there, which, from their age and form, I recognised as *ours*. I seated myself in an armchair covered with red velvet, and ornamented with gilt nails, such as I used to occupy in that very room long ago. Ah, what thoughts assailed me! Of my brother who, in the midst of this world's pomps, thought only of the happiness of his subjects; of my sister—that excellent Elisabeth, that angel upon earth—sent by monsters to heaven with the crown of martyrdom.

"Presently, in the midst of illusive memories which made me, for the moment, young again, I abandoned myself fully to a sort of vision of the past. Versailles appeared once more before me in all its former splendour, when suddenly I heard under the window cries of 'Vive le Roi!' 'Is the King going to hunt to-day?' said I to myself, forgetting, for the moment, that I was King. Thus roused, I remembered that it was the hour I had fixed to go on to Trianon. At Little Trianon memories of my youth flocked back to me in crowds. The same gardens, the same pavilions, where we played *comédies en famille.* It was in the village, on the banks of that pretty lake, that the Court used to abdicate its grandeur, in order to realise the projects of Don Quixote when he proposed to Sancho to find happiness in pastoral life. Here the beautiful Marie Antoinette was but a young farmer's wife: that dignified queen was, on occasions, the most charming of dairymaids. We never then guessed that a day would come when such humble conditions of life to which we descended for amusement, would in reality be envied by us. I remembered the brilliant fête which the Queen gave at Little Trianon to the Emperor, her brother, and the artistic and brilliant illumination of those delicious groves on that occasion. In the midst of them was the Temple of Love; and to light this up in a picturesque manner, fifteen hundred faggots were consumed. . . . . I wished to roam through the apartments, and in doing so was struck by the elegance of a bed draperied with muslin embroidered with stars of gold.

"'Who has occupied this bed?' asked I.

"'The Queen,' was the hesitating reply.

"'Oh,' answered I; 'but these hangings are too fresh not to have been arranged for some other occupant?'

"Then, at last, came the answer—'Joséphine!'

"Is Little Trianon, thought I, ominous to crowned women?

"Passing again through the garden," continued the King, "I perceived some *soucis*" (marigolds, emblems of sorrow and care) "growing near a beautiful tuft of lilies. This coincidence struck me; and whilst the crowd welcomed my re-appearance with joyous cries of 'Vive le Roi!' I murmured the first couplet of a song which often in exile had caused my beloved niece to shed bitter tears.

> "Dans les jardins de Trianon
> Je cueillais des roses nouvelles.
> Mais, hélas! les fleurs les plus belles
> Avaient péri sous les glaçons.
> J'eus beau chercher les dons de Flore,
> Les hivers les avaient détruits;
> Je ne trouvai que des soucis,
> Qu'humectaient les pleurs de l'Aurore."

CHAPTER VII.

MR. AND MRS. DRUMMOND—THEIR HOTEL IN PARIS—SINGULAR CASE OF NERVOUSNESS—LOUIS PHILIPPE, DUC D'ORLEANS—RECEPTIONS AT THE PALAIS ROYAL—LORD MILTOWN—COUNT D'ORSAY—THE POET MOORE—COLLEY GRATTAN—COLONEL D'AVISIER DE PONTES—BARON JAMES DE ROTHSCHILD—MR., MRS., AND MISS CANNING—GRAND BALL GIVEN BY THE MARQUIS OF SLIGO—MISS LUCY DREW—FETES AT MONTMORENCY—LORD CLANRICARDE.

CHAPTER VII.

WHEN in Paris, after the Restoration, I always stayed with my relatives Mr. and Mrs. Drummond, who occupied a house which had formerly belonged to the celebrated Madame Tallien; and to her notorious taste the general magnificence of that house and all its appointments was originally due. Mr. Drummond held various important appointments under the Allied Governments in Paris; and was not only Paymaster-General of all the troops, but Commissary-General to the whole of the Army of Occupation. Mrs. Drummond was a charming person, much younger than her husband, and still beautiful; but although her house was one of the best frequented in Paris, she was afflicted with such constitutional shyness that she never entered any large assembly without feeling for the moment as though blind and deaf. Habit, however, so well enabled her to appear conventional in manner, despite this insurmountable bashfulness, that one evening when I was with her at the Palais Royal, where we went to every Wednesday reception, the Duc d'Orléans conversed with her in English without discovering the peculiarity under which she laboured, though I who was standing near her had, now and then, to touch her as though to wake her up to the necessity of making some gesture of response; and yet all the time she looked so pretty, and smiled so sweetly, that the future King of the French could not but flatter himself that his conversation was peculiarly agreeable to a lady who, in fact, neither heard nor saw him.

The weekly receptions held by the Duc and Duchesse d'Orléans at the Palais Royal were largely attended. Bourbonists and Bonapartists were sometimes almost equally represented there; and while the Emperor Alexander was in Paris, he was almost always there with a number of Russian officers. There, too, we continually met Lord Miltown, who, I really think, had the handsomest face of any man I ever saw; but, having lost the use of his legs when quite a child, he always went through the rooms, either at the Tuileries or the Palais Royal, in a wheeled chair which he guided himself.

Count d'Orsay, Moore, and many other celebrities then in Paris, felt at home in Mrs. Drummond's house, and enjoyed the delightful gardens which belonged to it; gardens where choice flowers bloomed, and on the spacious lawns of which peacocks strutted, in a way to make visitors forget the vicinity of a large city. Grattan, who was at that time with Moore in Paris, used to tell me that he could never approach the hostess of this charming abode without fear; for to him she seemed like some rare ornament of Sèvres china, which he was afraid to touch, lest he might break it.

Small literary côteries used sometimes to form themselves in Paris in those days, in a way to make one think that, under the pedantic King Louis XVIII., the time of "Les Précieuses" was not altogether past.

I remember that a Colonel d'Avisier de Pontès one day told Colley Grattan that he was making a translation of Shakspeare into French, but that he found it necessary to expurgate the original text of the great English dramatist, as it was much too coarse for the refined taste of Parisians. Grattan shrugged his shoulders at hearing this; but Moore, who was also standing near, was about to interpose, when the Colonel suddenly turned round to him and complacently added, "Well, my dear Moore, I have been translating your 'Loves of the Angels;' but in that case also I was obliged to leave out a very great deal that is too gross for France." Moore, upon hearing this, seemed almost bursting with indignation. He glared at his translator furiously; and then, turning round to a pretty English lady and amateur poetess standing near him, exclaimed, "How I should like to throw that fellow out of the window!" This, however, was easier to say than to do, for Colonel d'Avisier was six feet high, and Moore was a dwarf in comparison with him, although broad and strong.

I used often to see Baron James de Rothschild, and I must confess that I liked the large balls given at his house much better than I liked its host. At one of these balls I first met Mr., Mrs., and Miss Canning. In later years Baron James de Rothschild improved exceedingly in his mode of entertainment; but at the last ball he gave, at that now distant date, in honour of the Allied commanders who were present, I, with many other of his guests, fainted; for a larger ball-room than his house contained being requisite, a spacious tent was erected in the grounds; but the smell of fresh paint in this temporary ball-room was so overpowering that the result was as already told.

Canning was so charming in society that it was a treat to me to listen to his conversation, even when it turned upon politics, which were beyond my comprehension. Sometimes when he was talking to Sir Charles Stuart and Mr. Drummond, I grew bewildered, for not at that time understanding aught of the doctrine of expediency in politics I was surprised at hearing men in power alternately praised or abused, not according to their own several merits or demerits, but according to the measures which it was either hoped or feared would be adopted by them.

Among the Restoration festivities in Paris, was a very splendid ball at the hotel of the Marquis of Sligo, who had been Governor in India. The rooms were crowded, but not to suffocation, for though the weather was overpoweringly hot, cold water was poured down continuously outside the house from the windows above those which opened into the principal ball-room. I do not know whether our host had learnt this mode of keeping up a fresh atmosphere in India, but I can testify to the perfect success of the plan adopted by him on that occasion in Paris.

There was a great deal of amusement that night in a little côterie, of which I for some time formed one, as to the mispronunciation of English names by the French. Sir John and Lady Knatchbull, for example, were sometimes spoken of as "Sir and Lady John Bull." Count d'Orsay, Lord Grey, Moore, and others of the circle round me, made merry at the then absurd appearance of English toilettes, the elaborate inelegance of which was in those days, when Paris and London had been so long politically and socially far apart from each other, strangely in contrast with the refined though perhaps coquettish simplicity of the dress of French ladies. My mother being French, I was always dressed according to her taste; but a young lady of our immediate party had, on that night, so overladen her dress with ornaments, that Moore and others entreated me to use my influence with her, as she was a friend of mine, to induce her to assimilate the fashion of her dress to that of the French.

This young lady, Miss Lucy Drew, was a niece of Lady Augusta Murray (married to the Duke of Sussex), and possessed not only beauty, but a fine intellect. She took the hint as to her toilette in good part, and even the wit for which she was previously celebrated, seemed improved thereby, for she afterwards became extremely popular in the literary circles of Paris. She was the daughter of Lady Susan Drew, daughter of Lord Dunmore (afterwards Lady Susan Douglas), and was allowed to receive guests, and to exercise her own somewhat fantastic tastes in the arrangement of her mother's house in a way quite unusual among French young ladies, but which was none the less in harmony with her own charming individuality.

We used often to make up parties with Lady Susan Douglas, Lady Clayton, and several other friends, French and English, to picnic at Montmorency, where we passed the time in riding through the beautiful wood on donkeys. Count d'Orsay, Colonel d'Avisier de Pontès, the Duke of Berwick, the three sons of Sir William Clayton, Moore, and Lord Clanricarde were the usual cavaliers in attendance upon these occasions, which sometimes were not without their own peculiar dangers.

One day in particular, I remember we all suffered greatly, for Miss Stuart, the daughter of Lady George Stuart, fell off her donkey, and as the animal still continued its pace at a great rate, and her dress had caught on the pommel of the saddle, she would have been seriously injured had it not been for her presence of mind, which enabled her to regain her footing the moment after her fall, and as it was not possible to extricate her dress, to run as fast as she possibly could by the side of the donkey; in fact, she was literally dragged onwards by it. The more speedily the donkey was pursued, the faster it went, and therefore the greater the danger for Miss Stuart still bound to its side; but a clever Frenchman at last rushed round in advance by another path, and by suddenly facing the animal, compelled it to halt; and Miss Stuart, in a state of breathless terror, but still uninjured in life or limb, was rescued.

Each lady riding on a donkey at Montmorency had a gentleman walking by her side; and on that day when Miss Stuart's accident occurred, Lord Clanricarde happened to be walking by mine.

I here particularly mention Lord Clanricarde, because, after the alarm had subsided, he amazed as well as amused us all by various gymnastic feats, some of which were remarkable; and I was told that he could run up to the top of a wall several feet high, without apparently touching it, or availing himself of any prop or support whatever. Another of his achievements which he did then was to put three donkeys side by side, but at equal distances from each other, and then, after having jumped over them successively, to leap over them all three together. This was a feat in which he might probably be rivalled by many practised in athletic exercises; but the following was more singular, and certainly astonished us all. When we had sat down to the luncheon prepared for us, Lord Clanricarde, wanting to change his place from one side of the large luncheon table to the other, took a flying leap across it, and landed on the other side, without the least injury to the bottles, or glasses, or dishes which were standing at the moment on it.

Many young Frenchmen of our party, and especially one brave aide-de-camp, who had already much distinguished himself in battle, were eager to imitate Lord Clanricarde's feats; but they all failed, one after the other—a source of much vexation to them, especially to the aide-de-camp, who could not be made to understand that in these performances there was a "knack," to say nothing of the necessity of long practice. Lord Clanricarde (who afterwards married Miss Canning) was only about twenty years of age at that time. He was a devoted admirer of Moore, and used to sing that poet's songs. He was full of life and spirits;

and on the day of this entertainment, his vivacity, excited perhaps by the successful display of his physical powers, led him to commit some practical jokes, one of which nearly got him into trouble.

After luncheon, we had all agreed to wile away the time before our return to Paris, by walking about in the lovely wood of Montmorency; and as the sound of music was heard in the distance, the whole of our party naturally wended its way in that direction. At last, on emerging from the thick shelter of the trees, and coming upon an open space, we found ourselves in presence of a group of French peasantry dancing. The scene was a pretty one; for the people were all dressed in their best and brightest coloured costumes. The women wore their coquettish white caps, everybody looked happy, and quadrilles and valses fast succeeded each other, danced in a way in which the French alone—albeit only French peasants—can dance.

All this was charming to behold; but all of a sudden we, looking on from a little distance, beheld Lord Clanricarde demurely approach the dancers, leading a donkey. After a pause of a minute or two, he took his place on the green sward, as though to form part of a quadrille which was proceeding, and forced the donkey to sit up on its hind legs by his side, declaring it to be his chosen partner. Instant signs of displeasure displayed themselves among the French people, and especially on the part of the male dancers, into whose midst he had thus imprudently intruded himself.

I was at the moment standing near his mother, Lady Clanricarde. Her fears were so excited for her son's safety, that she rushed forward and implored him to desist from his mad antics; but he would not listen to her. She then came running back again, more than ever alarmed, for the indignation of the peasants became every moment more and more manifest. Not knowing therefore what else to do, she turned to me and said—"Ah! you can speak French quite well; they will listen to you; go and quiet them." I approached the dancers, who were by this time becoming furious under the supposed insult offered to them by an Englishman; and I explained to them that the whole thing was only intended as a good-humoured joke. They listened to me, but they did not seem to appreciate the humour of the jest, nor to be at all appeased by my explanation, until, to his mother's great satisfaction, I succeeded in inducing Lord Clanricarde with his donkey to leave them.

CHAPTER VIII.

COLONEL D'AVISIER DE PONTES—PARTICULARS OF HIS LIFE—MATRIMONIAL ENGAGEMENT—PERPLEXING LETTER—SEVERE ILLNESS OF COLONEL D'AVISIER DE PONTES—HIS RESIDENCE IN LONDON—APPOINTED GOVERNOR OF ROCHELLE — UNEXPECTED VISITOR — THE VICTIMS OF TREACHERY AND DUPLICITY—UNHAPPY MARRIAGE—LOVE, LAW, AND RELIGION—DEATH OF MADAME D'AVISIER DE PONTES.

CHAPTER VIII.

IN the course of these reminiscences I have mentioned the name of Colonel d'Avisier de Pontès, and the memory of him is so intimately connected with those days at Montmorency, that I am here tempted to allude to a few remarkable particulars of his life.

In 1814-15 he was anxious to pay his addresses to a young lady who was extremely handsome and very rich. She, like all the world, had come to Paris after the Restoration, and at a number of balls and parties, whither she went with her mother, she constantly met Colonel d'Avisier de Pontès, whose marked attentions were evidently received by her with satisfaction.

Some time previously they had first met in Italy. He had never forgotten her, and as she had never ceased to remember him, it was no matter of surprise that, when he again encountered her in Paris and proposed to her, she consented to become his wife. Her mother, however, did not wish her to marry either a Roman Catholic or a Frenchman, and refused her sanction to the engagement. This was a matter of regret to the betrothed pair, but as the bride-elect was of age, and possessed of a large estate and considerable property quite free from maternal control, she refused to recall her bethrothal, but conceded to the wishes of her mother only so far as to postpone the date of her marriage until she should have accomplished a short tour through Rhineland in her company.

In about two months the mother and daughter returned from this tour to Paris, and then, when the latter again declared her inflexible determination with regard to her approaching union, her mother was compelled to yield, and the engagement was formally announced to the world.

The mother at that time behaved most kindly to her intended son-in-law, and he, not suspecting the sincerity of her seeming regard for him, consented to her wish that the wedding should take place in the native land of his betrothed—an arrangement which would admit of his previous introduction to the different members of her family.

With many promises of constant correspondence, the lovers parted, with the happy assurance that in a month's time they would be married. The bride elect and her mother came over to England, and the Colonel, after accompanying them on their way as far as possible, returned to Paris, there to obtain leave of absence from his regiment, and to make those arrangements which were rendered necessary by the changed mode of life which he confidently hoped awaited him.

By the earliest post possible after his parting with his fiancée a letter reached him in her well-known handwriting. Joyfully he tore it open; but what was his consternation when he saw it declared to him her determination at once to break off their engagement! "The difference of our religious opinions," so ran this cruel letter, "will be an insuperable barrier to true sympathy . . . . . . Do not write to me, for nothing will induce me to change my decision, and if you do write I shall burn your letters unopened. Do not attempt to come to me, for I will not consent to an interview with you. Try to forget me, or think of me only as a friend."

Colonel d'Avisier de Pontès was in despair when he had read the letter, which for ever crushed all his long-cherished hopes of happiness. He came to me, and in the greatest agony of mind, asked me if I could throw any light on the subject. Of course I could not do so, and indeed I was not less amazed than he was at the tone of this missive, for, as her friend, I had never for one moment doubted the earnest truth of her attachment to him. Not heeding her injunctions to the contrary, he did write to her a passionate appeal which might have melted a heart of stone, and he implored an interview, if only of a minute's duration.

But all in vain. Days, weeks, months passed away, and no answer came either to his agonized remonstrances and renewed pleadings for mercy, or to letters which I, who beheld this unhappy man dying from the effects of the cruel wound inflicted on him, took upon myself to write in his behalf to the woman whom he still so ardently loved. Once he crossed over to England in the hope of seeing her, but upon arriving at her home he was coldly and even rudely received by her half-brother, who told him that she was at that time on a visit at the distant house of a friend, and that it was by her own inflexible desire that all communication with him, her once intended husband, had ceased as it had done.

After this, Colonel d'Avisier de Pontès' state of health was so shattered that it necessitated a change of scene to Italy, and there he was stricken dangerously ill with brain-fever; but when convalescent from this attack, the miniature of his betrothed was ever kept near him, and looking upon the lovely eyes it portrayed, and upon the lips which seemed to smile upon him, he could not even then understand how the original of that cherished picture could be false or fickle.

Years passed, and when I saw him again in 1825 he was so sadly altered in appearance that I could scarcely recognise him. In the meantime he had devoted himself bravely to his military duties, but all the joy of his life had faded away. Afterwards when in London he used to pass a great deal of his time with Count d'Orsay, and at the house of Lady Blessington. He was also frequently in the society of Prince Louis Napoleon, who, when after many years he became Emperor of the French, showed his friendship for Colonel d'Avisier by appointing him Governor of La Rochelle.

A lifetime had thus gone by, when one night at La Rochelle, General d'Avisier de Pontès was sitting alone in his library, the door of which being suddenly thrown open by a servant, and a lady dressed in the deepest mourning appeared before him. Her veil was down, but when she found herself alone with him she flung it back, and throwing herself on her knees at his feet, looked up at him, saying—"Amédée, will you forgive me?"

It needed but the sweet tone of her voice, thus uttering his Christian name, to assure him that this woman kneeling before him was indeed no other than his once betrothed bride, and before he could command words in which to express his mingled delight and surprise, she went on—

"Amédée, forgive me. The misery of both

our lives has been caused by my want of faith in your love—a want of faith," she added, in a tone of shame and agony, "caused by the treachery of my own mother and sister."

He gently raised her and seated her where, still bewildered by her words, he could better behold her. It was indeed the long lost love of his youth, her lineaments changed by time, and still more by sorrow; but to his eyes still more lovely than those of any other woman he had ever seen. Presently, controlling her emotion as well as she could, she went on to tell him that, only a few days before, she had discovered the duplicity of which they had both been the victims. Her mother, she said, was just dead, and not until almost her last hour had she confessed to her that, in the far off time before their intended marriage, her letters to him had been suppressed, the one he had received being a forgery, and that his letters to her had been intercepted. She further told him how she had been made to believe that he was unfaithful to her, that he had renewed his acquaintance with a lady to whom he had formerly been attached, and had married this lady and gone to Italy with her. When she was told this frightful falsehood she was attacked by a dreadful illness, during which her agony of mind was so acute that, when life came slowly back again to her, fears were entertained that she would lose her reason.

With an infinite pity, born of the one only love of his life, General d'Avisier de Pontès continued to listen while the woman who ought years ago to have been his wife, the woman now once more seated by his side, proceeded to tell him how, after that one dreadful illness, five years of the sickness of sorrow ensued to her, until at last she had grown so listless in her indifference to all but the memory of himself that she was induced to marry a man who frequently visited at the house of her mother, but of or for whom she herself neither knew nor cared anything. Yielding to the solicitations of her family she became his wife, and not long afterwards she was awakened to the horrible consciousness of his real character by his ferocious conduct towards her in money matters; for her property having been settled upon herself, he was determined never to let her rest until by violent threats and various forms of cruelty he had wrested it all from her.

For some few years the burden of her existence under the same roof with this monster would have been utterly intolerable, save for the love which had sprung up in her heart towards a little daughter, who seemed as though sent by heaven to console her. To this child she clung in her misery, and continued to do so even after the child's father, having forced her (under threat of shooting her if she refused) to sign a cheque for 5000*l.*, had eloped with another woman to America.

A year had scarcely elapsed after this event when the child was taken ill with scarlet fever, and died. All hope then faded out of her heart. A deed of separation had been drawn up, which fortunately rendered it impossible for her cruel husband to return to her, but life was to her altogether a blank, until at last she was roused from the listlessness of utter despair by the illness of her mother, who on her death-bed made a confession, the truth of which was attested by her delivery to her of the key of a desk in which were contained the letters that years ago had been written, but which had never reached her until then, when her mother was pleading to her for forgiveness in the agonies of a last remorse. The forgiveness was granted; the mother was now dead; and she and the man who ought long since to have been her husband, were now again together, for she had lost no time after her mother's funeral in hastening thus to throw herself at his feet.

For a brief moment General d'Avisier de Pontès could scarcely believe in the happiness her presence caused him; but only too soon was he reminded that the wretch whose name she bore, the mother of whose child she had been, was still alive.

"If he is not dead," she exclaimed, "I have not heard anything about him for more than fifteen years, and have been legally divorced from him."

Then again did his sense of misery return, for, as a Roman Catholic, he could not marry a divorced woman.

Once more they were compelled to separate; but, as they trusted, for a short time only, for they determined at once to take the best legal advice upon their case that both Paris and London could offer.

In Paris the law seemed entirely against them, but in London both Lord Lyndhurst and Lord Brougham were inclined to a more favourable opinion. Lord Brougham at one time recommended General d'Avisier de Pontès to turn Protestant in order to facilitate matters, but this he declined to do. The woman, however, whom he had so long loved had not the same, or indeed any, objection to become a Roman Catholic, for her late Protestant mother's conduct was not calculated to impress her with much reverence for the bigoted scruples she had practically manifested in her treachery towards Colonel d'Avisier, on the ground of his being of a different faith to herself; but her becoming a Roman Catholic could not help them at all. After a great deal of consideration they at last determined to make an appeal to the Pope; and the decision of His Holiness was that her marriage could be dissolved if she became a Roman Catholic, as there had been false representations which had forced her to the union from which she sought to free herself.

It need scarcely therefore be said that she became a convert, and that her marriage with General d'Avisier de Pontès at length took place. After the marriage I often saw them. In 1855 he was visiting London, and frequently declared to me how thankful he was to Heaven that at last he had married the only woman he ever really cared for; adding, "What on earth can I have done to deserve such a blessing?"

Such happiness, however, is seldom of very long duration in this world, and people began in time to wonder at the reason why Madame d'Avisier de Pontès, who was still extremely handsome and charming, appeared but seldom in society.

At the Tuileries her presence was always welcome, and the Emperor Napoleon III., her husband's old and kind friend, wondered why she was only too often absent from the midst of the Imperial circle.

The truth, alas! was that long years of unmerited sorrow and misery had undermined her health more seriously than her husband wished the world in general to suppose, and a few years after she married the man from whom she had been so cruelly separated, she died in a convent, in a most melancholy state. I frequently saw her in her last illness, and the account of her trials, to which she was morbidly inclined to recur, was most painful.

CHAPTER IX.

ESCAPE OF NAPOLEON FROM ELBA—CONDUCT OF LOUIS XVIII. AT THAT TIME—MY FATHER'S INQUIRIES AT THE TUILERIES—NOTE TO MY FATHER FROM THE ARCHBISHOP OF SENS—EXCITEMENT IN THE STREETS OF PARIS—NAPOLEON'S ARRIVAL AT THE TUILERIES—HIS ENTHUSIASTIC RECEPTION THERE—MY OWN IMPRESSIONS OF NAPOLEON—CONVERSATION WITH QUEEN HORTENSE—MADAME DE CAYLA'S VISIT TO NAPOLEON.

CHAPTER XI.

IN the month of March, 1815, the star of Napoleon was once more in the ascendant. The Emperor had escaped from Elba; he "knocked at the gates of Grénoble with his snuff-box," and they opened to him; and in twenty days (from the 1st to the 20th of March) that strange prophecy was fulfilled which had declared that the Imperial eagle would fly without pause from steeple to steeple, even to the towers of Notre Dame.

Meantime, "Louis, by the grace of God, King of France and of Navarre," had addressed a proclamation to "his brave armies," conjuring them by all they held sacred (including His Majesty's own Constitutional Charter), and in the name of the Great Henri, to testify their fidelity to the Royal cause, warning them that France would not suffice for Napoleon, and that he would exhaust her population anew, to go to the ends of the earth in order to purchase fresh conquests with her blood.

But it was all in vain that Louis XVIII., gloomy and gouty, exerted himself to dictate the long and eloquent appeal containing these adjurations. Previous to dictating it, he had attempted to review the National Guard; but unfortunately His Majesty's health was not equal to his energy in this attempt. Anxiety had aggravated his sufferings from gout, and he was soon brought back to the Tuileries more dead than alive.

My father sent to the Tuileries to inquire of his friend and relative, the Archbishop of Sens, brother of the Marquis de la Fare, what were the intentions of the King, and whether he purposed leaving Paris, or remaining there. The Archbishop of Sens wrote to my father, in reply, "My dear Lord Maurice Drummond, Louis XVIII. will die in the Tuileries, but he will never leave them." The Archbishop, however, was not infallible, for the King did rally, as before said, sufficiently to dictate the proclamation to the "brave armies of France," and by the 20th of March he was so far recovered as to flee from Paris, and to leave the Tuileries ready for the reception of Napoleon.

Thus, after a restoration of eleven months, the Bourbons were again exiled.

From daybreak upon that evenful 20th of March, Paris presented a strangely animated scene. Detachments of cavalry were briskly moving in various directions; regimental bands were playing their most inspiriting music; and companies of infantry, passing to and fro, seemed elate and even triumphant, as though after some great victory. Carriages were driving about hither and thither at a most extraordinary pace, and—what was more remarkable—all of them were laden with luggage.

My father at last determined to go himself to the Tuileries, in order to ascertain the true state of affairs there, for the outside scene before him by no means coincided with what was written in the note which had reached him from the Archbishop of Sens. He went accordingly, and then it was he heard that Louis XVIII. had left the Tuileries with the Garde du Corps, and that many leading Royalists had likewise already fled from Paris.

Yes, Napoleon had arrived; or, in the words of the time, "The Little Corporal had come back again with the violets."

He had paused at Fontainebleau on the evening preceding; and now, on the 20th of March, the anniversary of his son's birthday, he was received in Paris with a frantic joy, which, venting itself in enthusiastic cries, caused the air to resound with "Vive l'Empereur!"

When he reached the Tuileries, he was "snatched from his followers (MM. de Caulaincourt, Bertrand, and Drouot), and was borne forward in the arms of the officers present to the top of the staircase." He was so overcome by his emotion at these evidences of ardent attachment evinced by those surrounding him on all sides, that he shed tears, tears of which until that moment many people had believed him to be incapable, and then walked straight forward, not looking on either side, but abandoning his hands to those who pressed forward to kiss them with overwhelming testimonies of affection.

My father had always found the Emperor, through the influence of Josephine, willing to oblige him; and now, when convinced by a look from Napoleon that he was not forgotten by him, he hurried home in order to give my mother and myself a chance of likewise beholding this extraordinary man upon that eventful day.

My mother was still in a state of too much alarm at all the exciting circumstances going on around her, to accept this chance; but as I had always felt a great desire to see the hero

> "Whose game was empire, and whose stakes were thrones,
> Whose table earth—whose dice were human bones,"

I accompanied my father back to the Tuileries. When we arrived there, the Emperor was addressing the soldiers and people from the balcony. The crowd was enormous, but, as if with one voice, it kept on shouting, "Vive l'Empereur!" Napoleon's words were eloquent, at least so they seemed to me, uttered as they were under an inspiration that was overwhelming. Every syllable, every action, of the speaker seemed to act with magnetic force on the hearts of the audience; and when at last his full grey eye chanced to light upon me, I felt as though it had power to read through my inmost soul at a glance.

The troops shouted with joy as he told them

that they should again march under the Eagle to glory—that emblem which had led them on to victory at Marengo, Jena, Austerlitz, and under which so many triumphs had been won—that emblem again upraised to avenge the insults which France had suffered from the Allies.

While Napoleon was uttering these stirring promises, which were received with cries of "Vive l'Empereur!" continually echoing far and near, the banner of the Fleur-de-lys was no longer floating over the Tuileries, for the tricolor was again in the ascendant.

But no wife, no child, welcomed Napoleon back, although, before quitting Lyons, he had written to his consort, Marie Louise, to inform her of his progress, and to forewarn her of his intention to make his triumphal entry into Paris on the 20th of March, the anniversary of their son's birth.

As he himself afterwards bitterly said, Joséphine would never have deserted him. But Joséphine was dead. Her daughter, Hortense, arrived at the Tuileries on the evening of the 20th. Under the title of the Duchesse de St. Leu, the Ex-Queen of Holland had remained in Paris with her two sons during the eleven preceding months of the Bourbon Restoration, and now that she was again in presence of the Emperor he at first seemed doubtful as to the motives which had lately guided her political conduct, and was evidently displeased at her having recently instituted a lawsuit against her husband (his brother Louis) by which the world at large had been informed of her unhappiness in her married life.

"I did not expect to find you here," said Napoleon, curtly, to Queen Hortense.

"I remained in France," replied Her Majesty, "to take care of my mother."

"But afterwards?" asked the Emperor.

"After her death," she answered, "I found in the Emperor Alexander a protector for my children, and I endeavoured to secure their future prospects."

Now Napoleon himself was under obligations to the Emperor Alexander, for it was partly due to the generosity of that Sovereign that the Duchy of Parma had been conceded to his son, the King of Rome.

He could no longer, therefore, blame Queen

Hortense for having accepted the protection of the Russian potentate in behalf of her children. "Let us say no more on these subjects," he exclaimed; then turning towards her he added, in a tone of emotion—

"And you were present with my poor Joséphine to the last! The news of her death amid our many misfortunes pierced my heart."

The Empress Marie Louise had never been popular in Paris, as Joséphine was to the last, nor had she the fine instincts which so especially distinguished the first consort of Napoleon, who was indeed his better angel. For example, one day Napoleon, having been provoked by her father, the Emperor of Austria, declared to Marie Louise that he was "an old *ganache*" (blockhead). Her Majesty asked one of her ladies-in-waiting, as she said the Emperor had called her father by that name, the meaning of the word *ganache*, and the lady, not knowing what to say in reference to the Empress's own father, answered that it meant "a venerable old man." Marie Louise believed this, and afterwards, when Cambacérès came to pay his respects to her, she, wishing to be very complimentary to him, said, "Sir, I have always regarded you as the chief *ganache* of France."

The Bourbons had suspected Queen Hortense of a share in a Bonapartist conspiracy; but, as Napoleon himself declared, there was no conspiracy, although Fouché, Duke of Otranto, the subtle minister of police, had attempted to league himself with her, as he had done with the partizans of Louis XVIII., and especially with the celebrated political intrigante Madame de Cayla.

Madame de Cayla remained for some time in Paris after the flight thence of Louis XVIII. As it has since been confessed, Fouché still visited her in disguise, and through his agency she subsequently joined the again exiled Monarch at Ghent; but this not until after she had been summoned to appear at the Tuileries. It will be remembered that the Comtesse de Cayla was by birth, as well as by personal sympathy, a Royalist, although by marriage she was incorporated into an Imperialist family. As nominally belonging to the latter, she had in former days been well acquainted with Queen Hortense, and indeed had, when at the Court of Marie Louise, excited the observation of Napoleon himself. The circumstances of her interview with the Emperor at the Tuileries were therefore so remarkable and so significant of the strange times in which it occurred, that an account of it, translated from her own description, can scarcely here be out of place.

"My relatives," says Madame de Cayla, "had flocked round their former master, and had been very well received by him. I know not if the sight of those gentlemen recalled me to the memory of Bonaparte, or if somebody had spoken to the Emperor of the confidence with which Louis XVIII. had honoured me; but, let the cause be what it may, I had a proof that His Imperial Majesty deigned to think of me. I received, in short, a note from Queen Hortense, whom I had not seen since the Restoration, notwithstanding her residence in Paris. She engaged me in the most amiable terms to come and pass the evening *tête-à-tête* with her. These words, which were underlined, made me understand that something mysterious was involved in this invitation, and I had too much experience in politics not to accede to it.

"Queen Hortense possessed the amiable qualities which had endeared her mother Joséphine to those around her, and a most enlightened taste for the fine arts, which she herself cultivated with much success. She excelled in landscape and flower-drawing; in a melodious voice she sang songs of which she herself had composed both the words and the music, either of which would have been pronounced exquisite even had they not proceeded from a Princess. The beauty of Queen Hortense has been much vaunted; but, although my testimony on this point may be suspected, I will sáy that she was rather a pretty than a beautiful woman. . . . . But she had so much grace and fascination, her figure was so noble, her manner so affable, and she dressed herself with such taste that she appeared more beautiful than she was.

"She at this time presided over the Imperial Court at the Tuileries, and provisionally occupied the place of Marie Louise, whose speedy return the Emperor announced to the Parisians, but they did not believe in it. I arrived at the hour fixed by the Queen. I found her alone amusing herself by looking at some engravings with a lady of honour, whose name does not recur to me. The Queen received me graciously, made me sit near to her, and, after some compliments, said to me, 'You have been fortunate. You have passed from the Court of the Emperor to that of Louis XVIII.'

"'It is true,' replied I, 'that I went sometimes to pay my respects to the Princes of the Royal Family.'

"'Very well! I do not wish to know more. But confess that you regret the Bourbons.'

"'I should be ungrateful,' replied I—'I should be ungrateful if I failed to remember the kindnesses with which they honoured me.'

"Just at this point of the conversation I heard the door of a neighbouring apartment shut violently, and then the sound of booted footsteps resounding on the floor. All those who have seen Bonaparte can affirm that in his gait and gestures there was something extraordinary; he was quite unlike every other man. In an instant I knew that he was in the adjoining salon. At this thought an inexpressible uneasiness seized me. I felt ready to faint, when we heard the sound of a handbell impatiently ringing. Queen Hortense rose.

"'It is necessary,' said she, 'that we pass into the next room. You will find somebody there who desires to speak to you.'

"This mode of summoning us by ringing so roused my indignation that it restored my courage, and yet I knew that it was an ordinary custom of Bonaparte to use this method of calling the members of his family. . . . . I rose. I followed the Queen, and I was in the presence of the Emperor. With his usual impetuosity he advanced towards me, and without making the least salutation to me, he took me by the hand and conducted me to an armchair.

"'Sit down,' said he to me.

"Then instead of seating himself also, he walked away with rapid strides to the end of the salon. When he came back, he said—

"'It is a long time since I have seen you, Madame. You are as pretty as ever.'

"'But, Sire,' said the Queen, 'Madame is of my age.'

"This interruption was singular, for the

Queen was five or six years older than myself; but I replied only by congratulating the Emperor on the excellent health he appeared to enjoy.

"'And have you no congratulations to offer to me on my return?' asked he.

"This repartee, and, above all, the look which accompanied it, confounded me. Bonaparte perceived this, and continued,—

"'Well, Madame, was Louis XVIII. very gallant?'

"I gathered up all my courage, and replied,—

"'I know nothing on that point, Sire; but I can assure your Majesty that he never abused the superior privileges of his rank to torment a woman admitted to his presence.'

"'Ah! I have vexed you,' he exclaimed, laughing. 'So much the better; that will avenge me a little for what you have done against me, notwithstanding that neither you nor yours had any subject of complaint against me.'

"'Neither have I ever uttered a complaint of your Majesty.'

"'No; but you have intrigued, caballed,

plotted, conspired with people of every colour, —emigrants, ideologists, republicans. See the fine service you have rendered to France! for, at last, in spite of you, here am I come back, and for a long time, I hope.'

"He pronounced these last words with an accent which, in all my life, I shall never forget. Then, after another rapid turn through the room, he suddenly began to ask me a thousand questions on the King, Monsieur, the Duc d'Angoulême, Madame Royale, and the Duc de Berry. He wished to know everything; their private customs, their relations with such and such persons of the former Imperial Court, particularly with M. de Talleyrand, the Abbé de Pradt, &c., the correspondence they had no doubt left in France, &c. It may be easily credited that I evaded a great number of these questions, and declared myself unable to reply to His Imperial Majesty concerning others.

"The Emperor often turned the conversation on Madame Royale, Duchesse d'Angoulême. for whom he expressed an admiration he was far from extending to other members of the Royal Family. He asked me afterwards if I was in the habit of seeing the Dowager Duchesse d'Orléans, who was detained in Paris by having broken her leg at the moment she was getting into the carriage which was to convey her from France. Upon my replying that I was rather frequently admitted to the honour of paying my court to her, he said,—'Well, assure her from me that I will raise no obstacle to her residing in Paris. Tell her, also, that I grant her an annuity of a hundred thousand francs from my privy purse. Official intelligence of this shall be sent to her to-morrow; and if that sum be not sufficient, the Duchess has but to write to me.'

"Having said this he took up his gloves, which he had placed on a side-table—perhaps, to let me see his aristocratic hands;—and, without a word of farewell to us, he went out.

"I had not thought that our interview would be thus occupied with details which were not only frivolous, but useless to the Emperor.

"I had thought that, through my mediation, he would have wished to open some negotiation with the fugitive Princes; perhaps, whilst chatting with me, he changed his mind, as he often did.

"This conference with the Emperor lasted three quarters of an hour; and I used the time and opportunity of closely observing my illustrious interlocutor. Here is the result of my observations.

"Bonaparte on that day wore a green uniform; and I have been assured that it was the same that he afterwards wore at Waterloo, and subsequently at St. Helena, although, by that time, old and almost ragged. In the morning he had been reviewing troops in the Champ de Mars: his coat, his hat, and his boots were still dusty. . . . . But in vain did I seek in his eyes that fiery and piercing glance which formerly illumined them. He stooped more than he used to do; his head was bent towards his chest; his complexion was sallow; his countenance sad and dreamy; and his little hat, crushed down almost to the eyes, increased their melancholy expression. His movements were still brusque, but by habit, and not by hot impetuosity as formerly."

CHAPTER X.

RETREAT OF LORD MAURICE DRUMMOND AND FAMILY TO VERSAILLES—A REPUBLICAN HOST—TERRORS OF WAR ENDURED BY US—ARRIVAL OF THE RUSSIAN AND PRUSSIAN TROOPS—MARSHAL NEY—RETURN OF NAPOLEON FROM WATERLOO—HIS LAST VISIT TO MALMAISON—THE SECOND RESTORATION—SOIREE AT THE PALAIS ROYAL—BLÜCHER—TALLEYRAND—FENCE OF WORDS BETWEEN LOUIS XVIII. AND THE GREAT STATESMAN.

CHAPTER X.

NOW that Napoleon was again installed at the Tuileries, my father thought that it would be prudent once more to leave France; but, finding that no British subjects were permitted to do so at that critical moment, he succeeded with difficulty in removing his family—consisting of my mother, my brother, my grandmother, and myself—to Versailles. There, in the Place d'Armes, we at last obtained apartments in the house of a man named Grincour, who in politics was a regular *Bonnet Rouge.* This fierce Republican, however, was not without natural sympathies; for when my father, who seldom used his eloquence in vain, represented himself as in a distressing position, considering that not only his wife and children, but his aged mother also, were under his protection, Grincour said,—"Well, I will make room for all your family. I am well known here: I shall go to the authorities and declare that you are my cousins just come from the country; and if inquiries are made, I am the only person in this house who will have to answer them."

From four large windows in our apartments, facing the Place D'Armes, we could see down the Avenues; and as day after day of "The Hundred Days" went on, we were at last continually hearing that Bonaparte was victorious, and had beaten the Allies. This continual state of excitement and suspense was very harassing; and indeed, their enforced residence at Versailles was full of sad associations to my grandmother and father. For looking at the Palace, now gloomy, deserted, sacked, and desecrated, they could not avoid drawing bitter contrasts between the past and the present times of their lives. Now full of anxiety for the future of France, as well as for what Fate had still in store for themselves, they could not fail to remember the once gay and brilliant Court wherein they had severally played a part, and the tragic end of the Queen who had been the bright centre of that Court.

One day we were startled by seeing a

number of Cossacks, scarcely human in their frightful appearance, galloping up the Avenue which led to the Place D'Armes. "Revenge! Revenge!" they shouted, "Remember Moscow!" And while these alarming cries resounded, cannon balls were flying, some of them literally striking against the house which held us.

The inhabitants of Versailles were seized with a panic of terror upon that day, for these Cossacks forced their way into all the shops, and consumed everything which they could devour. They even drank lamp oil, and fed themselves upon tallow candles, if no other provisions could be found; they forced open the doors of stables, in which they stalled their horses, and broke into houses, where they brutally insulted and outraged everybody. During the whole of the night that followed, a night during which we did not dare to go to bed, a horrible tumult prevailed, and above it continually rose shrieks and cries of murder.

In the morning we ventured to look out of window, and great was our joy to find that the Russians and Prussians had at last arrived, they having marched on through the hours of darkness. The Place D'Armes was covered with soldiers and officers lying down to rest; and when at length we heard that the Duke of Wellington and the English troops were likewise in France, we felt relieved as though from some hideous nightmare.

Soon, however, came a rush of French cavalry up the Avenue; they galloped into the Place D'Armes. Amongst them was Marshal Ney. The gates were closed; they tried to escape, but it was impossible to do so; and despite the heroic efforts of the Marshal, he was made prisoner, and conveyed to Paris; the fate that awaited him there is only too well known.

At last, when order was restored, and the Allies remained in possession, my father determined to return to Paris, but not, it will be believed, until he had sufficiently manifested his sense of obligation to our republican host, M. Grincour, for the shelter he had afforded us.

On the 22nd of June Napoleon abdicated.

At first, on his return to Paris from Waterloo, he had taken up his abode at the palace of the Elysée Bourbon. At noon, on the 25th, he left that palace; his carriage was drawn up within the grounds, that he might avoid the curious gaze of the crowd, but he could not altogether do so; he was recognised on his way, and cries of "Vive l'Empereur!" still greeted him; for the people scarcely realized as yet that he had nominally ceased to be their Emperor.

Napoleon bowed in acknowledgment of these salutations, but his countenance was impressed with care and sadness. Queen Hortense and her two sons (the younger, the now fallen Emperor of the French) awaited him at Malmaison, where Joséphine had died the year preceding, after the abdication which exiled Bonaparte to Elba.

Malmaison was to him full of memories, both painful and pleasing; his last conversations there with Hortense were continually of Joséphine; and when he thought of his absent but living wife and son, he felt, and again said, that Joséphine, whom he had divorced, but who had died because she could not survive his downfall, would never have deserted him.

No, Joséphine would never have left Napoleon to perish, unsoothed by domestic affection, of an agonizing disease, combined with the slow torture of despair, on an isolated rock—the "luogo tristo," as he called it, of St. Helena. It was there, however, that the fallen Emperor declared—"When Destiny wills, it must be obeyed;"—a creed which, however defective, gave him strength to conquer daily temptations to commit suicide, and still to declare that "Life is glory;"—a creed, too, which made him tolerant as to the deficient conduct of others towards him; for it was at St. Helena that he said of Marie Louise: "I believe that she is just as much a state-prisoner as I am myself, except that more decorum is observed in the restraints imposed upon her."

But I must now advert to Paris, after Louis XVIII. was once more restored to the throne of his ancestors.

After the second abdication and exile of Napoleon, and the consequent return of Louis XVIII. to the Tuileries, Paris presented a very gay scene. Balls and parties followed each other in quick succession, as they had done after the first Restoration. It was at a soirée at the Palais Royal, given by the Duc and Duchesse d'Orléans, that I first saw Blücher, and I gazed with more than ordinary interest at his ungainly person. Many years afterwards I met a General von Gräven, who had fought at Waterloo under him, and who told me the following anecdote concerning him :—

When the special messengers arrived to inform Blücher that Napoleon had escaped from Elba, and that his services would be immediately required in the field, they were astonished to find him literally running round and round a large room, the floor of which was covered with sawdust, and in which he had immured himself, under the delusion that he was an elephant. For the time it was feared that Blücher was hopelessly insane, or that he was so far suffering from *delirium tremens* that his active co-operation in the anticipated campaign would be impossible; but when the urgent news was brought him, he at once recovered himself, and proceeded to give his advice in a perfectly sound state of mind, the tone of which was thus, as by a sudden shock, restored to him.

General von Gräven also related to me a singular occurrence which happened to himself during the campaign in Belgium, and which I may as well record here.

General von Gräven, then a young man, and another cavalry officer, whose name I forget, were ordered by Blücher to proceed towards the battle-field with their respective troops, but to take different routes, the one to the right and the other to the left, as a precaution against the French, who were known to be on the watch.

General von Gräven went according to Blücher's directions, and when, after a long day's march, he came to a church, he determined that his men should halt for rest. As many of them as possible entered the church, where they found beds of straw but lately vacated, and various other tokens which showed them that the French had quite recently occupied the quarters of which they now took possession; and they were thus convinced that they must be in much closer vicinity to the enemy than they had imagined. Nevertheless, they flung themselves down to snatch a brief repose, and the General himself was so wearied with his late march that he soon fell sound asleep.

But, just at dawn of day he suddenly awoke, and there before him stood his friend, who had gone with his troops to the left, while he himself had taken the right, as already said. Great was the General's surprise at thus unexpectedly beholding him, but before he could find words to speak, the latter said to him in a distinct voice—"Do *not* follow orders: do *not* proceed on your present route; for the French have got possession of it, and are lying in wait for your approach."

The General sprang up to speak to his friend, but, to his amazement, he had vanished and was nowhere to be found. Determined, however, to take his advice, he forthwith awoke his men, and again set forth on his march, but by quite a different route from that originally designed. In due time he joined the Allies in safety, and then to his awe and horror he was told that his friend had been killed at the precise time at which he had appeared to him in the church, and that almost all the men under his command had been massacred, as undoubtedly his own troop would have been had he not accepted the warning he received.

Apropos of the soirées at the Palais Royal, I am reminded of many other celebrities whom I was in the habit of meeting there; but chief among them Prince Talleyrand stands forth in my memory, not only on account of his long friendship with my family, and his long unsuspected attachment to my Aunt, as mentioned in a previous chapter, but because, under a quiet exterior, he was incomparably the most brilliant conversationalist present. Every sentence he uttered was epigrammatic, and often pungent with satire; yet all the time that he gave vent to such utterances his smile was most pleasing; and I must add that, although then and long since quoted by the world as a mere dexterous diplomatist or heartless man of wit, that smile of his emanated from a goodness of heart for which few people but those who knew him well gave him credit. I have seen Prince Talleyrand weep as well as smile; it was upon a day at a later date than that to which this period of my narrative refers, when he told me how in his youth he had loved my aunt Emilia, and how Fate, which in the early years of his life had been too often antagonistic to him, had prevented his marriage with her.

Louis XVIII. did not like Talleyrand, and none the more so because he felt that his own somewhat pedantic conversation was overpowered by the Prince's brilliant intelligence. Sometimes a sharp though short encounter of words would take place between His Majesty and the great diplomatist; and one of these encounters I remember to have occurred on a Court day at the Tuileries when I was present. The King and the Duchesse d'Angoulême were both receiving that day; the rooms were almost full, and His Majesty appeared to be in most excellent spirits. Presently Prince de Talleyrand came in, and it was soon rumoured that he had asked for leave of absence from the King. Now everybody in Paris at that time knew that Talleyrand, though separated from his wife, was often threatened by her with the assurance that she would insist on taking up her abode with him, if he did not at once send whatever sums of money she happened to require. So the King, being in a merry mood, said, quite aloud, to the Prince, as the latter approached His Majesty, "Why,

Prince, I hear that as Madame de Talleyrand has just arrived in Paris you wish to leave;" and as Louis XVIII. said this he laughed, his laugh being of course echoed instantly by the numerous courtiers present who had heard his words.

But Talleyrand only bowed, and in a clear, sonorous voice replied, "Yes, your Majesty, it is my 20th of March."

It was then the King's turn to attempt to get up a laugh at his own expense, but he merely coloured and looked annoyed, for few things galled him more than an allusion to his flight on the date just named—a flight caricatured at the time in Paris by a flock of geese waddling out from the Tuileries, while eagles were flying in.

CHAPTER XI.

PROJECTED MARRIAGE FOR THE DUC DE BERRY—ENVOY TO NAPLES—ROYAL LOVE-LETTER—BRIDAL PROGRESS OF THE DUCHESSE DE BERRY—HER RECEPTION AT FONTAINEBLEAU BY THE KING AND ROYAL FAMILY—HER MARRIAGE—MY INTRODUCTION TO THE DUCHESSE DE BERRY—HER APPEARANCE—HER DAILY HABITS.

CHAPTER XI.

NOT long after the Bourbons were back again in France, it was proposed that the Duc de Berry, second son of the Comte d'Artois, should marry his cousin, Marie Caroline, Princess of Naples; for the Duchesse d'Angoulême (wife of the Duc de Berry's elder brother) being childless, there were fears that the dynasty, which it had cost so much blood and treasure to restore, would not be perpetuated to future generations.

The bride-elect of the Duc de Berry was granddaughter of Queen Caroline of Naples, and, therefore, great-niece of Queen Marie Antoinette. Her father (Francis, Prince Royal of Naples), was brother to the wife of Louis Philippe, Duc d'Orléans; she was, therefore, niece to Marie Amélie, Duchesse d'Orléans. Some coolness, on account of political suspicions on the part of Louis XVIII. towards

seen, by those who care to read it, in the following letter from him to her.

"Paris, Feb. 8, 1816.

"MADAME MY SISTER AND COUSIN,—I have long desired the King, your grandfather,* and the Prince, your father, to demand that to which I attach the happiness of my life; but before obtaining their consent, I would fain solicit your Royal Highness to deign to confide to me the happiness of your life in uniting it with mine. I dare to flatter myself that, by age, experience, and long adversity, I am not quite unworthy of being your husband, your friend, your guide. In quitting relatives worthy of your love, you will find here a family which will remind you of the time of the patriarchs. What could I tell you ot the King, of my brother, of *Monsieur*, and above all, of that angel, Madame, Duchesse d'Angoulême, which you have not yet heard, except that their virtues, their goodness, are far above any possible praises that can be uttered concerning them. . . . . . My relatives all

* King Ferdinand of Naples, who reigned sixty-six years, from 1759 to 1825.

eagerly desire that your Royal Highness may fulfil my wishes, and consent to augment the number of our family. . . . . Deign, Madame, to yield a favourable answer to my prayers, and to hasten the moment which will enable me to lay at your feet the testimony of the respectful and tender sentiments with which I am, Madame my sister and cousin, your Royal Highness's very affectionate brother and cousin,

"CHARLES FERDINAND."

The fact of this formal French love-letter being written proves that M. de Blacas had succeeded as a political emissary of Hymen to the Court of Naples. The banns of marriage were published at Saint Germain-l'Auxerrois almost immediately after the correspondence began between the royal bridegroom and bride elect; and on the 25th of April, 1816, the marriage by proxy was performed in the King's Chapel at Naples. Prince Leopold of Salerno represented the Duc de Berry on this occasion, and the Cardinal Archbishop of Naples invoked a blessing on the union in presence of a crowd of illustrious witnesses—who again assembled to assist in the grand festival of the royal bride's departure from Naples.

On the day of that event the people of Naples also flocked to the sea-shore to participate in it, and to testify their good wishes to the young Princess on her entrance into a new sphere of life and duty. Upon that amphitheatre, the unchanging scene of transient festivals and fears, a whole population surrounded the bride, and scattered flowers in her path as she was about to step forth from it. The clear air resounded with acclamations, and the blue, pure sky smiled at the short-lived felicities of earth, whilst Vesuvius loomed in one corner of the fair scene like misfortune, gloomy and menacing. But every thought of the young Duchesse de Berry was a hope as she set sail for France.

The reception of the Neapolitan Princess at Marseilles was enthusiastic. A detachment of Royal Guards awaited her there as an escort; also her lady of honour, the Duchesse de Reggio, with other members of her appointed suite. When she left the vessel which had conveyed her to the shores of France, she entered the port in a gilded boat, conducted by twenty-four rowers, dressed in white satin and blue and gold scarves. The royal bride was seated under a canopy of crimson velvet, fringed with gold, and surmounted by a crown of colossal proportions. Sheltered by the royal standard, floating in the soft summer breeze, and displaying the arms of France and of Navarre, the Princess advanced through a forest of ships, gay with evergreens and streamers, and when she stepped on shore the enthusiasm which greeted her was unbounded. The National Guard and troops of the line formed a passage for her progress through the streets of Marseilles: all the houses were decked with flags and garlands: and not only every window was occupied, but the roofs were thronged with people. Bells pealed, cannon roared, and music played. The welcome given the year of her birth by her grandparents at Naples to Horatio Nelson, seemed to be renewed, as regards all details of splendour, in that awarded in 1816 to the bride of the Duc de Berry at Marseilles.

According to diplomatic custom, the Hôtel de Ville of that city was, on this occasion, declared by a royal speciality to be neutral territory, and there the Princess was delivered by the Neapolitan ambassador and the noble Italian envoys, who had thus far accompanied her, into the hands of the Duchesse de Reggio, her lady of honour, and the other members of the illustrious household which the King of France had appointed for her. Louis XVIII., the Duc de Berry, and other members of the Royal Family awaited the arrival of the bride at Fontainebleau, for, by royal etiquette observed on this occasion, the King himself must introduce her personally to her husband. But the Duc de Berry wrote to her daily, and she frequently to him, during her progress through France.

In one of these letters, the expectant bridegroom says:—" . . . . I will not write you a long letter to-day, having much to send you that will interest you more. I am occupied in seeking horses for you, and I hope to find some that will suit you. We have been to see the *corbeille* (wedding garments) which the King gives you, and I hope that you will be content with it; it contains, above all, a ball dress that I shall be enchanted to see you wear. My father superintends the arrangement of your library. My brother and his wife

(Duchesse d'Angoulême) deck your chamber; each one of us finds a sweet pleasure in doing something that may be agreeable to you! And who more desires this than he already united to you by ties the most sacred? I am always afraid of my thirty-eight years of age. I know that at seventeen I thought those very old who were getting near to forty. I do not flatter myself that I shall inspire you with love, but rather with that tender sentiment stronger than friendship, that sweet confidence which ought to ensue from affection. I see that I finish not on this point. . . . Adieu, still fifteen long days! I kiss the hand of my wife as I love her.

"CHARLES FERDINAND."

And again he writes:—

"Fontainebleau, June 12, 1816.

"Your letter from Lyon, which I received from the hand of the King, has caused me a pleasure which I cannot express to you. I am charmed to be scolded by you about my writing; you have much reason to find fault with it; but, in writing to you, my heart carries me away, and you have no idea of the effort I am obliged to make to be legible. I experience also a great pleasure to-day—I possess your portrait. At least that does not do you injustice; and even were it a little flattering, one may be extremely agreeable without being so pretty as that portrait."

In a previous letter from Lyons the bride had written to the bridegroom :—

"Once for all, Monseigneur, count on my tender gratitude, and be certain that nothing escapes my sensibility; you have touched it deeply. You are content with me, say you, Monseigneur? It is, doubtless, to re-assure me that you say so, for I feel that I am wanting in much—very much—to be what I would to please you, and to realize the too flattering idea which has been given to you of Caroline. Believe in her good heart, in her desire to respond to your confidence, by according you hers entirely; that is all I can answer for to you: your care, your goodness, will supply the rest. I am extremely sensible of all that is being done to embellish my abode, and to array my person. How testify to you all my gratitude? You will help me, Monseigneur: I try already to need no interpreter when face to face with you, for I tell you very frankly that you are dear to your

"CAROLINE."

On the 14th of June, the Duchesse de Reggio, travelling in the same carriage with the bride, said to her:—"Madame la Duchesse de Berry is in the forest of Fontainebleau."

The emotion of the young Princess was naturally very great when at last she was about to behold the Prince to whom she had already plighted her faith, and with whose destiny her own was already inseparably interwoven. She looked round her on a scene, once beloved by Henri IV. and Louis XIV., in all its Summer beauty; and beneath the majestic trees of the forest which shaded her way, she beheld here and there crowds of people who had assembled to see her pass.

At last, in an open space towards which she was approaching, she saw before her two pavilions in the form of tents, ornamented with the double escutcheons of France and Naples. Then Madame de Reggio spoke again. "I ought to forewarn Her Royal Highness," said she, "that we are about to arrive at the Cross of Saint Hérem. It is there that Madame the Duchesse de Berry will find the Royal Family."

A few minutes more, and the carriage stopped.

"The King," continued Madame de Reggio, "advanced towards Her Royal Highness." The bride alighted from the carriage, but the etiquette established by the precedent observed in the ill-fated marriage of Louis XVI. and Marie Antoinette, interposed as a check to her eagerness. On the turf was extended a carpet, one half only of which she was to traverse, whilst the King, conducting the Royal Family, was traversing the other half. But the young Princess was only seventeen years of age; and in her the vivacity of youth, which her adopted people had already declared "quite French," was combined with the impetuosity of an Italian. She stepped on the carpet: but instead of pausing halfway, in the place assigned to her, she darted across the boundary, and flung herself at the feet of the King. The aged monarch was charmed by the impulsive grace with which the ceremonial of the occasion was thus overstepped, and hastened to raise the blushing young Princess, and to present her to her husband.

"My nephew," said the King to the Duc de Berry, "it is my daughter that I give to you, for already as a father do I love her."

The bride was then kindly greeted by Monsieur the Comte d'Artois, her father-in-law; by her husband's brother, the Duc d'Angoulême; and most tenderly of all, by the Princess she had come to supplant—Madame Royale, Duchesse d'Angoulême—who was called by the King his "Angel of Consolation," his "Antigone," and of whose saintly virtues and heroic deeds the bride had heard, ere she now looked for the first time into that noble face, on which early sorrows had left an indelible impression of sadness, but which was irradiated not only by the sublimity of self-sacrifice, but by the soft expression of womanly affection and sympathy when smiling a welcome on the young stranger.

When Madame Royale was just the age of this sister-in-law who embraced her, she was released from solitary imprisonment in the Temple to find herself an orphan and an exile; and the advent of this light-hearted being who now claimed her protection, was the signal to the nation at large that she herself had resigned all hope of perpetuating the ancient race of which she and her husband were both lineal descendants.

In all the marriage festivities celebrated in honour of the arrival of this her rival, the Duchesse d'Angoulême was compelled by her position to take a prominent part. When the bride made her grand public entry into Paris, it was Madame Royale, Duchesse d'Angoulême, who was seated in the same carriage with her and the King; and when the marriage ceremony was solemnized at Notre Dame on the following day, June 17th, it was she who helped to hold the canopy over the heads of the bride and bridegroom, while for them the blessing was invoked which had been denied to her,—the blessing of children. The void of a childless marriage was a peculiar trial in the case of the Duchesse d'Angoulême, who at that time, when she stood by the side of the young bride, her sister-in-law, was regarded as the future Queen of France.

All the splendour of ancient royalty was revived at the ceremonial of this marriage. Not since the marriage of the Duchesse d'Angoulême's own parents—Louis XVI. and Marie Antoinette—had such a display been made on such an occasion.

Not long after the marriage of the Duchesse de Berry, I was introduced to her. Although an Italian, she had a beautifully fair complexion; and in figure she was so slight that she looked almost a child. Her eyes were large and prominent; but though of a lustrous blue, there was an uncertainty in the expression of one or both of them: I say, *uncertainty*, because the effect of this expression could scarcely be called a squint.

She was, at that time, but a child-wife, with no anticipation of the sad destiny in store for her; and often when her husband returned to the Tuileries or the Elysée, after a brief absence from her side, she would break away from the courtly circle by which she was surrounded, and run downstairs to meet him, just for the pleasure of being carried up again in his arms.

Sometimes, on a wet day, she would place a number of chairs in a row, and amuse herself by jumping from one to the other.

Previous to her arrival in France, and indeed during his exile in England before the Restoration, the Duc de Berry had notoriously formed domestic relations for himself; but after his marriage with this vivacious little Neapolitan Princess, he was quite devoted to her.

CHAPTER XII.

COUNT MAURICE DE LA FARE—AN ANCIEN REGIME COURTSHIP—LORD MAURICE DRUMMOND'S LOGE AT THE THEATRE OF VERSAILLES—DIFFERENCE OF CONVENTIONS IN FRANCE AND ENGLAND—N—— M'C—— —MR. P—— — SINGULAR NARRATIVE — MR. P—— —THE MYSTIC MARTIN—DOCTOR ALIBERT—MYSTERIOUS INTERVIEW WITH LOUIS XVIII.—THE COUNT DE LAVALETTE—SINGULAR PREDICTION.

CHAPTER XII.

IN a previous chapter I have already alluded to my father's friend and relative, the Archbishop of Sens, Grand Almoner of Louis XVIII., and I may now mention that soon after our arrival in Paris, in 1814, that ecclesiastical dignitary had arranged with my father and mother for a marriage between his nephew and myself. My parents were then, and occasionally afterwards, resident at Versailles, and Count Maurice de la Fare, the Archbishop's nephew, and my *fiancé*, used to come to their house as often as he could, for he was one of the Garde du Corps quartered at Versailles. At one time I was almost daily in his company, and yet our love-making, if so it could be called, was of the most restricted character possible; for my mother, being a Frenchwoman, and still clinging to her *ancien régime* notions of etiquette, would have been shocked at any young lady speaking to, or seeing, her betrothed husband except in the presence of a third party.

Count Maurice de la Fare was the grandson of my father's old friends, mentioned in an earlier chapter, who had indulged him in some of his youthful frolics when in garrison at Metz; and doubtless the memory of those past times made him the more readily consent to my marriage with one of the family, though it was by no means a union to be desired with regard to matters of property. Impediments respecting the latter caused the marriage to be postponed from time to time, so that my engagement lasted for years (until the year 1819), and yet all this time, as before said, we might have been perfect strangers to each other, had it not been for an ingenious device of Count Maurice. Though not allowed to converse, we were permitted to sing; and sometimes he would bring a new song for me to try, the printed words of which were interlined in pencil with what he had to say. This song he would afterwards take away, but not until I had read the words he had written.

My father was, I think, inclined to be more indulgent than my mother in this affair, for, although likewise adhering rigidly to the restraints prescribed by old French convention in such matters, he would frequently take me to the theatre at Versailles with him—his old taste for the drama having by no means become extinct—and there Count Maurice used to join us, until at last the fact of his doing so became so much a matter of course that almost every evening he occupied a place in our box.

This practice, however, by no means tended to his military advancement, for it was during this period that his captain in the Garde du Corps, to whom I had never spoken, but whom I saw frequently at the theatre in a box that commanded a view of our own, sent the Abbé de Barjenton to my father with a proposal for my hand. This proposal was of course declined on the plea of my previous engagement. The captain at once arrived at the conclusion that the Count was my *fiancé*, and from that time forth the latter was placed under arrest for every trifle, especially when it was suspected by his superior officer that there was any chance of his meeting us at the theatre.

Count Maurice de la Fare was very handsome, and I believe that he was as sincerely attached to me as it was possible for him to be to one of whom in truth, though he sometimes saw so much, he knew so little. Be this as it may, circumstances, involving family considerations of property, over which we neither of us had any control, prevented our marriage. It was, therefore, perhaps, fortunate for both of us that the strictness of the conventions which so encompassed us that neither of us thought of breaking away from them, had precluded the possibility of our discovering a fund of sympathy and sentiment for ourselves, and being made wretched by the fact of our long and ultimately frustrated engagement.

Very different was the case of a young acquaintance of mine about that time in Paris, who had been educated according to the more independent rules of social life in England. Her name was N—— M'C——. She was the daughter of General M'C——, and had come to Paris on a visit to some friends. She was beautiful, but in such delicate health that there was something almost painful in her extremely fragile appearance. She was nevertheless much admired, but she steadfastly refused every offer of marriage. One of the pretenders to her hand was Colonel Arbuthnot, who was much attached to her, and would have been in every way a suitable match; but she recoiled from all attention, and still kept growing thinner and paler. The fact was, she had been engaged to Mr. P——, a son of a late Prime Minister, and was still earnestly devoted to him, although, to all appearance, he had deserted her; for week after week, month after month passed, and he did not come to join her in Paris.

The cause of his neglect soon became known. After the departure of N—— M'C—— for Paris, Mr. P—— happened to be thrown a great deal into the company of Mlle. d'E——; and at last he became so fascinated by her, that, forgetful for the moment of former ties, he wrote to her one evening, beseeching her to accept him as her husband. The letter was sent, and in the morning he hoped to receive an answer to it. Meantime he lay down to rest, thinking thereby to still some pangs of conscience which already began to assail him. Sleep came to him at last; but after a few hours he was suddenly awakened from it; and, to his astonishment, he beheld N—— M'C—— standing by his bedside, in the midst of rays of light as clear as those of day. He saw her, but not as when he had last parted from her, for then she was bright with the bloom of youth and beauty, but now she was pale and wan,—the ghost of her former self. The vision, the phantom, or whatever it was, faded away; but the effect of this apparition on the mind of Mr. P—— was such that, without waiting for an answer from Mlle. d'E——, he rose, and started next morning to Paris.

Arrived there, he lost not a moment in seeking an interview with N—— M'C——, and found her exactly as she had appeared to him so mysteriously. All his old love came back to him at the sight of her; and with it a sentiment more tender, if possible, still. Anxiety, remorse, gratitude for her constancy, each and all took possession of him by turns. Henceforth Mlle. d'E—— was nothing, could never be anything to him; and in six weeks they were married.

A remarkable change, however, had taken place in Mr. P—— since that night of the vision, for he became as serious in mind and manner as formerly he had been gay and thoughtless; and when he returned with his wife to London they both became Irvingites; and with Mr. Henry Drummond (father of the Duchess of Northumberland) and Mr. Paul, devoted himself to a prayerful life of charity.

Mr. Paul was married and in the army, and had led a worldly life. Being attacked by a serious illness, the doctors in attendance upon him declared that it was impossible for him to recover, and retired from what they believed to be his deathbed with the assurance that they were unable to do more for him.

Mr. Irving, Mr. Drummond, and Mr. P——, however, took possession of him. No more medicine was administered to him, but constant supplications were offered up by his bedside. Sometimes the worshippers would remain almost all night in prayer to Heaven; and in confirmation of their own belief in the efficacy of faith, though to the surprise of everybody else, Mr: Paul recovered.

Mr. P——'s story was a remarkable one, but even Louis XVIII., albeit a *soi-disant philosophe,* was not without some belief in supernatural influences; at least, so it may be supposed from the following fact, which was no secret at the time of its occurrence in Paris.

Early in the year 1816, a husbandman named Martin, of the market-town of Gallardon, near Chartres, was at work in his field when a young man of rare beauty appeared to him, and said, in a sweet voice, "Martin, go seek the King, and tell him that his Government is in danger."

Martin, though awed at the moment by this apparition, appears either to have entertained some doubts as to its reality, or to have distrusted his own capacity to fulfil the mission assigned to him, for he made no effort to obey its injunctions. Somehow, however, he was eventually made to understand that the vision was that of the Angel Raphael, who reiterated the command for him to repair to Paris, there to present himself before the King, and to say to His Majesty that which he would be inspired to say. It was even predicted that he would shortly be summoned to appear at the Court of Louis XVIII.

Martin, bewildered by the prediction of unexpected honour thus thrust upon him, and scarcely realizing what sort of spirit he had to deal with, invoked the aid of the Curé of his parish, who, not less mystified than himself, applied for advice to the Bishop of the diocese; and the end of it was that Martin was sent to Paris, but with a letter addressed to the Minister of Police, and under the special escort of a gendarme.

Fouché had been placed by the French Chamber at the head of a Provisional Government after the battle of Waterloo, and was subsequently reinstated in the police by the King; but his duration of power was short, and M. Décazes was then Minister of Police. Décazes was not less sceptical than his predecessor Fouché; and suspicious that there was some attempt to practise fraud upon him in this affair, he ordered poor Martin, on his arrival in Paris, to be at once lodged at Charenton, there to be examined as to his sanity by M. le Docteur Pinel.

At Charenton, however, the celestial visitant again revealed himself to Martin, "in all the splendour of seraphic glory;" and the husbandman, whilst bitterly complaining of the sorry plight in which he found himself through his attempt to obey supernatural orders, succeeded at last in convincing Dr. Pinel that, to say the most, he was only affected by "an hallucination," which could scarcely perhaps be called insanity.

The hospital students thought that the best cure for him would be a shower-bath, and one day they ruthlessly let down the torrents from one on his head; but the Archbishop of Rheims, hearing of the affair, was inclined to regard not only the hospital students, but also Dr. Pinel himself as mere materialists, and declared that the case ought to be still further investigated. Meantime the celestial Raphael fulfilled his predictions through the King himself, and that by simple means.

Louis XVIII. was subject to fits of increased gloom after his second restoration to the throne, and needed diversion. Having heard of Martin from Décazes and others, His Majesty's curiosity was excited; and, something in the spirit with which the Emperor Alexander of Russia was in the habit of consulting the mystic Madame Krüdener, the King asked Madame de Cayla (who afterwards made known the story)—"What do you think of it?"

Madame de Cayla's own curiosity had been roused concerning Martin, and therefore she unhesitatingly answered—

"Sire, it is essential that you see him."

The Court physician, M. le Docteur Alibert, was of the same opinion; for he was one of the most *spirituel* of the sons of Æsculapius, and was scarcely likely to neglect "moral remedies" in the case of a Royal patient who needed amusement. So Alibert felt the King's pulse, and said—

"Sire, I have not seen this visionary myself, but from what I have heard, I believe that there is something very remarkable in his madness—if indeed he be mad. Sire, none other but your Majesty can decide as to whether this man be sane or insane, for he affirms that he could prove his mission to the King of France by revealing things that are known to none else."

"But, Doctor," said the King, "do you admit the possibility of an apparition?"

"Sire, I admit everything which could prove that Heaven is occupied with your Majesty and the fortunes of France."

"But, Doctor, you elude the question: Do you believe in apparitions?"

"Sire, I believe in the persons who believe in them. Faith makes everything possible. If Joan of Arc had been incredulous she would not have delivered France from the English,"

"No doubt. But," added the King, "there was no Academy of Sciences then to analyze miracles. Nevertheless, I will see Martin; that will divert us, and, if necessary, we shall refer to you, M. le Docteur Alibert, to attest that it is from your advice, and not from that of the Archbishop of Rheims, that we accord an audience to this visionary."

Still more to screen himself against the appearance of credulity, the King arranged so that Décazes, the minister of police, himself should conduct Martin to the Tuileries, and that the Master of the Ceremonies, the Marquis de Dreux Brézé, should introduce him privately into the Royal presence. Madame de Cayla, placed in a confidential *cachette*, was allowed, unseen, to listen; otherwise, as Louis XVIII. and Martin were left alone together, the following account of the interview might never have been recorded.*

The King was seated in an arm-chair at a table when Martin entered, ushered in by the Marquis de Dreux Brézé, who then withdrew. His Majesty was profusely decorated with the orders of Royalty, possibly with a view to test Martin's *sang-froid*, and it was probably also for the purpose of inspiring him with awe by the sight of regal magnificence, that, on his way to the room where the King invited him, he had been conducted through the state apartments of the Tuileries. But he entered the Royal presence without any token of embarrassment.

Martin was dressed in a coat of coarse grey serge, leathern gaiters, and hobnailed shoes; but he advanced quietly towards the King, and bowing, said, "Sire, I salute you."

---

* This interview took place a short time before the marriage of the Duc de Berry with the Princess Marie Caroline of Naples, and the chief prophecy refers to the assassination of that prince, of which some particulars are given in an after-page of this work.

"Good day, Martin," replied His Majesty. Hearing himself called by his name, the peasant seemed still more at his ease. The King told him to take a seat, thinking perhaps that the man would say with more freedom whatever he had to say if placed in an easy position. Be this as it may, Martin availed himself of the King's permission (possibly not knowing how extraordinary it was), and addressing His Majesty said—

"You know, Sire, why I come?"

"I have been told," replied the King, "that you had something to communicate to me. What is the purport of your journey?"

"Sire," said Martin, "I am sent by the Angel Raphael, one of the great powers of Paradise. He has appeared to me several times, telling me that I ought to present myself to the King, and that once alone with him, he would inspire me with the useful counsels that good souls have besought of him in their prayers in behalf of your Majesty."

"Well, speak!" said the King.

"Sire, you have been betrayed, and you will be so again."

"The throne, is it shaken? Which is

menaced—my person, or my family? Is it death or exile that is to be feared?"

"Death will come at its appointed time," said Martin. "But the prayers of your exile have been granted; you will have a tomb at St. Denis."

"In fact," said the King, "I more frequently demanded the tomb than the Crown of my forefathers."

"Heaven in mercy has listened to you, but you have not done enough for our holy religion. You lean for support on men, and they have betrayed you—some by their incapacity, others by their wickedness—for the demon of pride and impiety was their god. At this moment the negligence of those who serve you encourages your enemies. The prison doors themselves open for your captives."

"You speak of Lavalette?"* asked the King.

---

* The Count de Lavalette (Marie Chamans), born in 1769, of obscure parents, was educated for holy orders in the church, "but although for some time he wore the habit of an abbé he became a lawyer." During the Revolution he was an officer in the National Guards: and afterwards, serving in the armies of the Rhine and of Italy, he won the confidence of Bonaparte, who not only entrusted him with his secret correspondence but gave him in marriage to Emilie de Beauharnais, niece to Joséphine

"I know not his name," said Martin.

"No matter. But who has achieved the prisoner's escape?"

"Sire, the slowness of pursuit denounces those who ought to have prevented it."

"But women, Martin, who wish to deceive us are more subtle than the police."

---

by her first marriage. During the Consulate Lavalette was made Count and Commander of the Legion of Honour, and after various successes under the First Empire he showed much energy in accelerating the return of Napoleon. In 1815, when Louis XVIII. fled from the Tuileries, Lavalette assumed the direction of the Post Office. The consequence of this was that, when Louis XVIII. was again restored to the throne of France, Lavalette was condemned to death as an accomplice of the Emperor. He was thrown into prison, but he escaped, disguised as his own wife. To explain the possibility of this, it may be said that Lavalette was somewhat feminine in appearance. He had (says the Duchesse d'Abrantès) a pretty little white hand, two little eyes, and an immoderately little nose placed in the midst of a very fat pair of cheeks. The locks on his head were so carefully trained that by the wits of the staff they were each nicknamed; such as the *invincible*, the *redoubtable*, the *courageous*, and one especially, which defied the discipline to which the others were subjected by their owner, was called the *indomitable*. But notwithstanding his peculiar personal appearance and his dandyism, Lavalette was much respected by his friends, his foes, his children, and his wife. The latter, who was of extreme beauty when he married her, was afterwards somewhat disfigured by the small-pox. Lavalette showed the greatest delicacy in not allowing her to fancy from his conduct that she was at all changed in appearance, but the idea that she was so overshadowed her life with a profound melancholy.

"Yes, Sire, but mistrust those who serve you. Peace in the home department will not be restored to France but in 1840. Until then conspiracies will undermine the throne; a hand sharpens a poniard!" The King trembled. "A hand sharpens a dagger!" continued Martin. "Hasten to multiply the young plants, for it is willed to stop the sap in the branch that buds. Misfortune has already blighted one; it is necessary to graft that which can still ornament the old trunk with foliage and fruit."

The King understood that in this figurative language allusion was made to his nephews, the Ducs d'Augoulême and de Berry, and to his niece, Madame Royale, and he answered—

"But, as the angel who sends you, is the same who married young Tobias, and delivered his betrothed from demons, could he not render all the branches of the tree fruitful?"

Martin had become animated in his words. An *air de prophète* had stolen over his whole appearance, and the King, as if fascinated, was profoundly attentive to his conversation. It was therefore with no laughing interest that His Majesty awaited the reply to his last question: "Cannot all the branches of the tree be made fruitful?"

"Sire," said Martin, "the decree is irrevocable."

"But," resumed the King (alluding to the Duc de Berry and his left-hand marriage in England)—"But a wife and children already exist—a legitimate union. Ought we to recognise it?"

"Sire," was the answer, "you speak not all your thought. You would not wish a conjugal alliance with the enemies of France and the Catholic religion? Follow your inspiration, it is good; the dagger will come too late; a baptism of blood is preparing, *but life will be born from death!*"

"We fall into the Apocalypse," said the King, striving to shake off unpleasant impressions. But at a later date he had too much cause to remember this prediction.

"Sire," continued Martin, "the result will enlighten you. But haste! *the day of the dagger is written.*"

Other predictions uttered Martin. At one time the King looked upwards as though in prayer, with his hands clasped together in the form of a cross. At last Martin asked His Majesty's permission to return to his native home, adding that it had always been announced to him that no harm should happen to him.

"Neither shall any happen to you," said the King; and then His Majesty rang a bell. M. Décazes presented himself, and received orders to entertain Martin hospitably till the morrow, when he was to return to his home unmolested.

The rustic was led off by Décazes, and now that his mission was accomplished he asked permission to look over the palace. His desire was accorded, and several courtiers encountered by him on his way through the various apartments, seeing the respect paid to him by the Minister of Police, supposed him to be some illustrious personage who for the moment chose to be *incognito* beneath the coarse garb of the husbandman.

But when it transpired that Martin had made revelations to the King, all sorts of conjectures were formed. Was he an agent of the Jesuits? Or had he come to tell His Majesty that the Dauphin had *not* perished in the Temple? This was believed by many.

The nine days' wonder, however, gradually ceased to be one; but in after-years, as a subsequent page will show, there was only too much cause in Paris to remember the mystic Martin.

CHAPTER XIII.

MONSIEUR DÉCAZES—BARON VON S—— —BARON BARBIER —M. THELLUSSON—LORD MAURICE DRUMMOND—A CHALLENGE—A DAUGHTER'S PERPLEXITY—CURIOUS CONVERSATION WITH BARON VON S—— —STRANGE CONFESSIONS —MR. DRUMMOND'S LETTER.

CHAPTER XIII.

M. DÉCAZES, in whose company Martin made his exit from the presence of Louis XVIII., was not always on the right official track in his Argus-like search for offenders against the Government; and this I can prove by narrating a not unimportant circumstance in my own life.

After my engagement with Count Maurice de la Fare had been broken off, several proposals were made for my hand; but, as I had no preference for any of my would-be suitors, I begged my father to decide for me. Only too soon, however, I regretted my professed indifference upon a point of such importance to myself, for Baron von S——, an Austrian, was recommended to me as a husband. He was very rich, his fortune being more than 300,000*l.*, and his income amounting to at least 15,000*l.* a year from the funds and landed estates. To all this I had no objection; but the owner of so much wealth was short, ugly, middle-aged, and had a strong German accent. Baron Barbier, the German ambassador, said that Baron von S—— was of a very good family, but he knew nothing about his wealth.

M. Thellusson, the famous French banker, and my father's friend, said that the Baron undoubtedly possessed the wealth of which he professed himself the owner, as he had great part of it in his own safe financial hands, but he knew nothing about his family.

With Baron Barbier thus on one side, and M. Thellusson on the other, the double fact of good birth and great wealth was proved. I had nothing, therefore, but my own personal objections to oppose to the projected match, and these I feared to plead beyond a certain point; because, according to my mother's French notions, a daughter ought to submit to the will of her parents in forming a first alliance; and also because I dearly loved my father, who evidently much desired my union with the Baron.

My dislike to the latter was nevertheless

so unconcealable that my father, perceiving it, hardly knew what to do, when, in about two months' time, the marriage-settlements were brought for his approbation. And what distressed him more, and added greatly to his embarrassment, was that Baron Weber (a foster-brother of Marie Antoinette), a gentleman of seventy years of age, who was a frequent visitor at our house, gave an account of his countryman which was quite unfavourable. In my inexperience I foolishly thought to reconcile all difficulties on the subject by expressing my willingness to marry him, but at the same time my determination not to reside with him. My father at first possibly attached no importance to this avowal of my resolution, but the idea having gradually dawned on him that circumstances might some day induce me to separate from the Baron, he determined to have a settlement made on me in case of such a contingency.

So, one day when the marriage-deeds were again under discussion, my father turned to his son-in-law elect, and said, "Well, Baron, I wish you now to tell me what you intend to settle on my daughter in case of her dislike to live in Germany with you?"

But the Baron replied, "I do not marry in order to live separate from my wife; and therefore I should not think proper to settle anything upon her if she did not choose to reside with me."

My father, who was very passionate, replied, "Do you really think my daughter would marry an ugly ape like you, unless, if she chose, she could live independently of you?"

The Baron rushed out of the house; and in the course of the evening a letter was brought for my father. He was fortunately not at home when it was delivered. My mother and I both recognised the Baron's handwriting on the cover; dreading mischief, she opened it, and inside we found a challenge.

A friend who was with us at the time, when she heard the contents of the Baron's letter, declared that, to prevent danger, she would go at once with me to the *Commissaire de Police*. So we ordered the carriage, and off we went. We found the *Commissaire* at his post, and showed him the challenge; told him that the person to whom it was addressed knew nothing whatever about it; and that he must exercise his official power in preventing the prosecution of the affair, as otherwise we dreaded the worst consequences.

The *Commissaire de Police* assented to our wish, and immediately ordered guards to be stationed at the Baron's door, with orders to prevent his exit.

I then went on a visit to Mrs. Drummond, who was still in Paris, and the Baron wrote to me there that the insult he had received from my father was such that nothing but his death or my marrying him could put a stop to his revenge; and that, although restrained from fighting at that moment, he, with pistols in his pocket, would follow my father wherever he went, in case of my refusing to become his wife.

I was much alarmed, and in my sore perplexity asked Mr. Drummond's advice on the subject. The answer was that, if I could possibly make up my mind to do so, I had better marry the Baron, as there were many advantages in such a marriage to counterbalance my reluctance to it. As the subject now presented itself to my view only under one aspect, that of anxiety for my father's safety,

I wrote to the Baron, expressing my consent to marry him, and he, having given his word that he was not going out for the purpose of fighting, was allowed to come to me at Mrs. Drummond's house.

I was in tears, walking up and down the room, when he arrived. At sight of him I felt inclined to rush away from his presence, but Mrs. Drummond, who was present at the interview, prevented me from acting in so imprudent a manner; beseeching me at the same time to repeat to him what I had just told her, as she was sure that he would then listen to reason.

Then I mustered courage enough to tell the Baron that I did not like him; that it was impossible for me to regard him with aught but dislike; that my father was aware of this distaste on my part, and that it was only natural that he should have done as he had done. My tears still flowed, but they had quite a different effect on the Baron from what might have been expected, considering the words I had ventured to address to him, for he exclaimed—

"I loved you before this, but now I adore

you; and nothing in the world will make me give up our marriage."

After this I had nothing to do but to submit to my destiny; I had secured my father's safety, but at a sacrifice which had rendered my own existence miserable.

No kindness on the part of my intended husband seemed to have power to touch me, though, particularly in one respect, he acted with the greatest generosity. Being taken seriously ill not long after the renewal of my engagement with him, he told Mr. Drummond that, to prevent all difficulty in my inheriting his wealth after he died, if his illness should prove fatal, he had withdrawn his money from M. Thellusson's Bank; that he had executed a legal document which would secure my instant possession of it; and that he had written a letter to me with full instructions how and where to obtain possession of all his property. My brother, who was then still a mere lad, but quite old enough to understand the purport of such a conversation, was also present at this interview.

The Baron, however, did not die, and preparations for our marriage rapidly succeeded his recovery.

My father, who had been kept in ignorance of the challenge which had never been delivered to him, and not, therefore, knowing the real motives of my conduct, was angry with me for what he deemed my inconsistency. I still continued to stay at Mrs. Drummond's, and there the Baron visited us daily, although I hardly ever spoke to him.

Things went on thus until the Saturday before the Wednesday which was fixed for our marriage. The trousseau was ready; the carriage was prepared in which we were to drive off, after the ceremony, on our way to Germany; and there seemed no longer any possibility of escape for me.

Upon that Saturday there was a large dinner-party, in the English style, at Mr. and Mrs. Drummond's. The Baron came up to the drawing-room almost immediately after the ladies had left the dining-room, and entreated Mrs. Drummond to persuade me to grant him a few minutes' private conversation at the other end of the drawing-room. Mrs. Drummond came to where I was sitting, and told me to converse a little with the Baron, saying,—"As you are to marry him, you may as well be more civil."

So I walked obediently to the sofa on the other side of the room, where he awaited me; but even then I shuddered at the discordant tone of his voice directly he began to speak, though he seemed surprised and delighted to find me prepared to listen to him. He began by saying,—"You never allow me to speak to you, so that you really do not know me?—Have you ever read 'Jacques le Fataliste'?"

I answered—"No."

"Well," he continued, "that book proves that what is to be must be; our marriage was written in heaven, and, therefore, it will take place."

Afterwards he added, in a tone of self-adulation, but with a voice as harsh as before, "You don't know me; you don't know how clever your future husband is."

Of course, to this I could make no answer; and then either by the force of self-conceit, or from sheer incapacity to understand the vast difference (according to other people's perceptions) between cunning and talent; or under a belief that I should be still more bound to him, if convinced, beyond the possibility of doubt, of the magnitude of his wealth, no matter how acquired, he almost petrified me into attention by disclosing the fact that the amount of money which he possessed was mainly due to nothing more nor less than a fraud upon Government. His statement abbreviated was this:—

Prince Metternich's estates were seized by Bonaparte when he took possession of everything available down the Rhine. When the Bourbons were restored to France, Baron Barbier was instructed by the Prince and other claimants to demand the revenues due to them from the time when the estates were kept by France, but this without success on the part of Baron Barbier. Baron von S—— was aware of this, and he consequently wrote to Prince Metternich and the other claimants, and told them that if they would place their claims in his hands altogether, independently of the Ambassador or any one else, he would undertake to bring them to a speedy and satisfactory conclusion, as he knew people in office, and how to deal with them. This was in 1820.

Full power was accordingly given to the Baron, and in various ways he acted upon it. He went to the Bureau, well knowing the clerks there, spent some few thousand pounds in bribery, and frustrated all subsequent inquiries from the Ambassador by purchasing silence and co-operation on the part of those whose payment depended on his ultimate success. Having, at length, managed to get all necessary papers into his hands, he sent in the claim; and three months afterwards he received the whole of the money. To Prince Metternich and others he forwarded the full amount that was due to them, and received, not only letters of thanks in return, but many praises for the diplomatic skill with which he had acted.

"But now to explain to you how I got so large a sum of money for myself," added the originator of these transactions, when narrating them to me with chuckling self-satisfaction. "Now, to explain. I made up the claim to last April (1820), and the stupid French Government paid me up to the date at which I sent in the claim, instead of only to 1814, the date of the Bourbon Restoration. Sixty thousand pounds a year, and six years over the real time! I pocketed the amount of those six years over and above what I had to pay to others, and this amounted to more than 300,000*l.* The sum of 30,000*l.* I paid to the clerks who had served me so well."

I was speechless with horror and amazement at this revelation. He thought that I was struck dumb by admiration at his cleverness. It was, therefore, with even an increase of self-confidence that he continued,—"Your father and mother will be present at our marriage; but from the church-door we drive off on our way to Germany, and you will never see them again. Your brother," he added, condescendingly, "may come to pay us a visit whenever you like, but my brothers you will never see, for we are not friends."

Spell-bound, I still continued to sit silently in the same place. I looked and felt, perhaps, as though I were in a dream; but, in truth, I was trying hard to remember every word of what had just been told me.

Presently, when the Baron and all the

rest of the company had gone, both Mr. and Mrs. Drummond, observing my abstracted air, came up and asked me what was the matter. I then told them the whole conversation, exactly as it had taken place, and stated the names of the clerks who had been accomplices in the transaction. Mr. Drummond wrote down the whole of what I repeated, and told me that, not long since, there had been printed placards out in every direction, offering great rewards to any person who would give such information as would lead to the discovery of somebody who had been guilty of a fraud on Government, which had discovered that vast sums of money had been paid in mistake.

Very early the next morning, Mr. Drummond went to the Baron (taking with him a witness), and showed him the memorandum he had made of his conversation with me. The Baron denied the whole thing, and declared that I had made an entire mistake; but Mr. Drummond knew that I was quite incapable of inventing the statement which I had made to him much more circumstantially than, at this distance of time, I can write it here. He, therefore, soon after returning home, sent a letter to the Baron, saying that I should not be visible that day, and warning him that the affair, which had recently formed the subject of their conversation, must be investigated.

This letter, however, never reached Baron von S——, for he fled from Paris an hour after Mr. Drummond had called on him, and was never there seen or heard of again.

CHAPTER XIV.

THEATRES OF PARIS—TALMA—MLLE. GEORGES—MLLE. MARS—EXCITEMENT AT HER APPEARANCE—MLLE. DUCHESNOIS—BAL DE L'OPÉRA—SIR NIEL CAMPBELL—HIS PERPLEXITY AT ELBA—DANGEROUS PRACTICAL JOKE—MISS CAMPBELL'S EXCUSE—CARNIVAL TIME—THE DUC DE BERRY—DINNER WITH THE KING—THE OPERA—THE TRAGEDY—LAST WORDS OF THE DYING PRINCE—ROYALIST SORROW AND ROYALIST HOPE.

CHAPTER XIV.

THE theatres of Paris possessed many attractions during the first few years succeeding the Restoration. *Realism*, as it is now commonly called, was as yet comparatively unknown either in dramatic art or popular literature, French or English. Victor Hugo was then only just about to place his foot on the first step of the ladder of fame; Talleyrand had not yet declared, as he did soon afterwards, that Lamartine was "the poet of the soul;" Chateaubriand had conceived the idea of his "Genius of Christianity," but then he had ministerial duties to perform in the King's Cabinet; the name of Balzac, the realist of romance, was as yet in the shade, and that of George Sand was not to be heard of as the idealist of literature and politics until many years afterwards.

Madame de Staël had exclaimed, "Be free, be virtuous; respect that which you love;

seek immortality in love, and divinity in nature; sanctify your soul as a temple, and the angel of noble thoughts will not disdain to enter therein." Madame de Staël, banished by Bonaparte, had reappeared in Paris—that city which she loved—since the Restoration; but it was not in her day that god-like kings and antique heroes went out of fashion in the theatres of Paris, nor had people then and there learnt to weep for themselves in the course of a tragedy of every-day life, such as Victor Hugo and others of his contemporaries contrived in time to place before Parisian audiences. But though the French stage was still "stilted" in its style, it was at an epoch immortalized by the acting of Talma, Mlle. Mars, Mlle. Georges, Mlle. Duchenois, and others whose names are not so well remembered by me. Talma bore a strong personal resemblance to Napoleon I., and imitated him in manner as much as possible. This likeness in style to the Emperor was not so wonderful, as it is well known that Napoleon had taken lessons in elocution from Talma; therefore one may say that the Emperor had imbibed Talma's manner, who had made a complete change in tragedy, and studiously avoided all the pompous stage attitudes then still in vogue. Unlike his confraternity at that time, who all turned out their toes like dancing-masters, he walked naturally; and while they invariably turned up the hand when giving an order on the stage, he pointed downwards, — the more impressive way of the two—which had been the style of the *ancien régime*. It was generally reported that Mlle. Georges was much admired by Napoleon, and if so, it only verifies the fact that small men are generally attracted by large women, for this actress was almost colossal in stature, and her voice was sepulchral in tone.

The voice of Mlle. Mars, on the contrary, was extremely sweet; in appearance she was lovely, and in movement she was grace personified. It was while the Allies were still in Paris that I first saw her. When she came on the stage, she was covered with bouquets of violets. She was a Bonapartist; the violet was the flower of the Empire; and so offensive was the sight of it that night to the greater part of the audience (including the Bourbon Court), that the generally popular actress was received with hisses. Some, however, were present who began clapping their hands ; and others quickly following the example, a perfect uproar ensued, in the midst of which the melodious tones of Mlle. Mars could not make themselves heard. Bouquets were showered down at her feet; though whether by her own friends or the friends of the Empire, it would have been difficult to say; but whatever the public irritation caused that night by her first appearance, adorned with the Imperial flower, the excitement gradually subsided before her superb acting, and as the piece proceeded, the applause due to her genius was unanimous.

Mlle. Duchesnois afforded, perhaps, in one sense, a greater proof of histrionic power than did even her contemporary just named, for she had to contend against a want of personal beauty. She was plain; but so electric was the charm of her mental gifts, so strangely radiant their power, that when once she became thoroughly animated by their exercise, she seemed transformed, and looked positively beautiful.

The Bal de l'Opéra was not improper in those days, and was a favourite amusement, in which the English in Paris frequently joined; and here, before referring to the more serious events of the time, I am tempted to tell a somewhat ridiculous experience of mine with regard to one of these entertainments.

Sir Niel Campbell and his sister were among a large party that went one evening to the Bal de l'Opéra. The ladies all wore black dominoes, but the gentlemen had no disguise.

Sir Niel Campbell had been appointed by the English Government to attend Napoleon during his exile in Elba, and so well had his duties been fulfilled there that the Emperor had had no fault to find with England as to the treatment he received during his sojourn on that island. But when at length Sir Niel had reason to believe that Napoleon was meditating the escape which he subsequently effected, he gave notice of his suspicions to the Government, soliciting at the same time the necessary aid and authority to prevent the *dénouement* which eventually took place.

The English Government took no adequate

notice of Sir Niel's representations. Either the importance of his information was doubted, or else, as was afterwards believed by some people, there was a studied purpose in treating such information lightly, for the original treaty between the various European powers and Napoleon, on his abdication, had been drawn up so hastily that its imperfections could only be rectified by allowing it to be broken, in order that a second and more secure one might be substituted for it.

Be this as it may, Napoleon escaped notwithstanding all Sir Niel's precautions to the contrary, and when the latter went with us to the Bal de l Opéra he was on his way through Paris to London, there to force an admission for which he had been some time waiting in vain—namely, that it was by no fault of his that events had turned out as they had done.

Sir Niel Campbell and his sister were in the habit of visiting daily at the house of Mr. and Mrs. Drummond, where I was staying, and consequently I saw a greal of them. I respected Sir Niel extremely, and felt much interested in the circumstances to which I have just briefly alluded; but in a sentimental point of view I had never for a moment regarded him in any other light than as the brother of my friend, his sister. Great, therefore, was my astonishment when, on that night, he began speaking to me in more glowing language than the terms of our acquaintance warranted, and before I had recovered from my surprise at some of his remarks, he crowned it by drawing a letter from his pocket and asking me if I did not know my own writing?

Taking the letter from his hand I was obliged to confess that the writing resembled mine, but at the same time I declared to him with truth that I had never written it, nor indeed had ever addressed a single line to him in my life. I reiterated this declaration, but nothing I said seemed to convince him. Such doubt on his side was sufficient to rouse my indignation, and I do not know what would have been the result of our argument had not his sister called me to her, and confessed that she was the writer of the letter in question, an indiscretion for which she implored my forgiveness. "For," said she, "my brother was low-spirited and miserable. I knew he liked and admired you, I wished to do something to

of view I had never for a moment regarded him in any other light than as the brother of my friend, his sister. Great, therefore, was my astonishment when, on that night, he began speaking to me in more glowing language than the terms of our acquaintance warranted, and before I had recovered from my surprise at some of his remarks, he crowned it by drawing a letter from his pocket and asking me if I did not know my own writing?

Taking the letter from his hand I was obliged to confess that the writing resembled mine, but at the same time I declared to him with truth that I had never written it, nor indeed had ever addressed a single line to him in my life. I reiterated this declaration, but nothing I said seemed to convince him. Such doubt on his side was sufficient to rouse my indignation, and I do not know what would cheer him, and although I began this jest in fun, yet when I perceived the pleasure the supposed fact of your writing to him caused him, I was tempted to proceed."

This was the sum of the explanation given by this only too devoted sister, and as it was less satisfactory to her brother than it was to me, we remained intimate friends.

Sir Niel Campbell soon afterwards left Paris for London, and thence was sent out almost immediately (as Governor) to Sierra Leone. Six months afterwards I heard, with great regret, of his death.

A time of public mourning was then at hand for the Court, and indeed for the people of France. On Sunday, the 13th of February, 1820, the Duc de Berry was dining with the King at the Tuileries.

The Prince was in high spirits, and made His Majesty laugh more than once at his animated description of a splendid ball at which he and his wife had been present the night preceding, for it was carnival time in Paris, and the gaiety of the Royal Family generally was represented by the Duc and Duchesse de Berry. They themselves had lately given two very brilliant entertainments at the Elysée, and all Paris was still talking of the taste and magnificence displayed on those festive occasions, while the condescending hospitality of the Royal host and hostess had made them more popular than ever.

During the winter months preceding Carnival the Duc de Berry had received various threatening anonymous letters, and at the beginning of February his death had been announced in London; but, whatever influence these sinister circumstances may have had on him, His Royal Highness was apparently forgetful of all but the Carnival amusements which had lately diverted him as he dined, chatted, and laughed with his uncle the King on this Sunday, which, as already remarked, was the 13th of February. He shared a superstition of the time that the number 13 was ominous to him, but, despite the warnings he had received, he took no precautions; and, after amusing the King with his conversation, declared his intention of going that night to the Opera. His Majesty retired, as was his habit, into his own apartments after the dinner hour at the Tuileries. The Comte d'Artois went his way, and the Duc and Duchesse d'Angoulême theirs.

I was at the Opera that night. The pieces performed were the *Carnaval de Venise, Le Rossignol*, and *Les Noces de Gamache*. A large audience was expected, and as the evening advanced the house was crowded. All the spectators were in gala dress, and the boxes were filled with notabilities and ladies in full evening costume, brilliant with flowers, and glittering with diamonds.

Brightest of all was the Duchesse de Berry as she entered, accompanied by her husband. The Duc and Duchesse d'Orléans were also present, and during an *entr'acte* the Duc and Duchesse de Berry left their own *loge* to visit them. The public then beheld the Duc de Berry caressing the children of the Palais Royal with almost paternal fondness, especially the little Duc de Chartres, who was his favourite, and through whose fair hair he frequently passed and repassed his hand.

Presently, before the end of the last piece (*Les Noces de Gamache*) the Duchesse de Berry, having slightly struck herself against the open door of another box in returning, complained of fatigue and proposed to retire. It was then a few minutes to eleven o'clock. The Duc de Berry rose to accompany her to her carriage, but he intended to return and see the last act of the ballet.

The Royal Academy of Music in those days was an isolated building with a street on each side of it. The entrance used by the Royal Family was in a side street called the Rue de Rameau, after the composer of that name. The carriage of the Duchesse de Berry was drawn up before this entrance. The carriage-door was open; the guards under the archway, and the sentry outside, were presenting arms. The sentry had his back turned to the Rue Richelieu, and the Comte de Choiseul, aide-de-camp to the Duc de Berry, had also his back turned to the same street. The Comte de Mesnard, first equerry of the Duchesse de Berry, presented his left hand to assist her in ascending to her carriage; whilst the Duc de Berry offered her his right hand. The Comtesse de Béthusy, in waiting on her, had just entered the carriage after her. The Comte de Clermont-Lodève, gentleman of honour to the Duc, was standing behind him.

One of the footmen had just put up the carriage-steps, and the Duc de Berry waved his hand and called out joyously as he stepped back, "Adieu, Caroline! We shall soon see each other again!" He had half turned round to re-enter the theatre, when a man, coming from the Rue Richelieu, glided unnoticed between the sentry and the persons surrounding the Duc, laid one hand on his left shoulder, and with the other stabbed him in the breast.

The action was so instantaneous, that those nearest to the Duc de Berry knew not for a moment what had occurred; for the Comte de Choiseul, fancying that the man had accidentally knocked against His Royal Highness, called out, as he pushed him aside, "Take care what you are doing!" The man fled, and the Prince cried out, "I am assassinated!" Then, clutching hold of the dagger which was still buried deep under his right breast, he exclaimed still louder, "I am a dead man; I hold the dagger." MM. de Choiseul and de Clermont, the sentinel, one of the footmen, and others, immediately darted off in pursuit of the assassin. He fled towards the Arcade Colbert, but it was reserved for a boy—a lemonade seller, named Paulmier, and a soldier of the Royal Guard, to capture him.

Meantime, the Duchesse de Berry had heard her husband's cry of pain. In her eagerness to reach his side, she nearly flung herself out of the carriage; but Madame de Béthusy held her back while the steps were let down, and a footman came forward to assist her. Not waiting, however, for any sort of formality, she sprang over the steps, calling out, "Leave me alone! I command you to leave me alone!" In a moment afterwards she stood by her husband, and received him in her arms as he sank back, having just withdrawn the poniard from the wound, and given it to M. de Mesnard. They seated the Prince on a bench in the passage entrance of the theatre, and made him lean against the wall. They unbuttoned his shirt to seek the wound. The Duchesse de Berry sank on her knees before her husband; she strove to stanch the blood as it flowed copiously when the clothes were removed. The Prince then again said, "I am dying—a priest! Come, my wife, that I may die in your arms." The Duchesse de Berry threw herself upon him, and clasped him to her heart, as he fainted. She was covered with his blood.

The assassin was now brought in to the Corps de Garde of the Opera-house; and M. de Clermont, first addressing him, exclaimed, "Monster! by whom hast thou been urged to commit such a crime?" But the only answer that could be obtained was, "The most cruel enemies of France." M. de Clermont thought at first that this answer betokened a confession of conspiracy, but he was soon made to understand that it was only intended as an insult to the Royal Family.

The soldiers who surrounded the assassin were so enraged against him, that there was some danger of their taking the law into their own hands and killing him on the spot; but MM. de Mesnard and de Clermont cried out to them not to touch him, as it was still thought that his revelations would prevent further mischief.

Whilst this was passing outside, the Duc de Berry had been conveyed to the little salon, or ante-chamber to the Royal box, within the Opera-house. He had recovered consciousness, and was again able to speak. His first words were, "Is it a foreigner?" And when answered in the negative, he said, sadly, "It is very cruel to die by the hand of a Frenchman." The Duc and Duchesse d'Orléans had been apprized of the frightful event which had happened, and (although the rest of the Opera audience knew nothing of it as yet) they hastened to join the wounded Prince and his distracted wife in the salon behind the Royal box. The anguish of the Duchesse de Berry was beyond any human power or sympathy to soothe; it is possible that she was even more unconscious than her husband of the presence of those relatives, when they entered pale and distressed, and with whom only half an hour since she had been conversing gaily. Her whole attention was concentrated on her husband; her eyes were riveted on his countenance, over which the pallor of death was already stealing. Two medical men, MM. Blanchaton and Drogart, were in attendance on him, as he reclined on an arm-chair, with the wound on his breast visible, and she, kneeling by his side, her lately gay and glittering costume stained with his blood.

The ballet was still going on. The sounds

of the joyous music of the *Carnaval de Venise* echoed in the narrow compartment where death and desolation had taken up their abode. The fatal news, however, soon spread; messengers were despatched to the Tuileries and to the Elysée. The dances and the music of the Opera ceased; the crowd left the theatre, appalled, though scarcely as yet knowing why or wherefore. Another crowd began to enter the theatre, as the public left it. First of all came the father of the wounded Prince, Monsieur, the Comte d'Artois. He was a very tender father, and loved his younger son and his daughter-in-law with the deepest affection. In prayer the Comte d'Artois sought relief for the pain and sorrow which he now shared and witnessed.

Priestly aid was at hand; but Monsieur had also summoned his own surgeon, M. Bougon, who applied his mouth to the wound to encourage the outward flow of blood from it. He most likely knew the risk he ran in doing so; but, whether or not, the Duc de Berry, though now beginning to speak with difficulty, was more anxious for him than he was for himself. "What are you doing?" asked the

Prince, endeavouring gently to push him away. "What are you doing? The wound, perhaps, is poisoned." And to the other surgeons the Prince said, "I am very sensible of your care for me; but you will not be able to prolong my existence: my wound is mortal."

The Duc d'Angoulême, and Madame Royale, his wife, soon arrived. The Duc d'Angoulême and the Duc de Berry were greatly attached to each other, and the interview between these two brothers on that fatal night was heartrending.

Madame Royale stood silent and motionless under this new sorrow. Her arms were crossed on her breast, and she is described by one who beheld her on that fatal night, as "the Angel of Misfortune weeping over the past, the present, and the future."

The dying Prince began to be anxious for the arrival of the King, for he yearned to gain pardon for the man who had stabbed him.

This Christian forgiveness of enemies had long since been instilled into the mind of Madame Royale by her father before his martyrdom; and surely now again had she cause to murmur the words she had left inscribed on the wall of her cell in the prison of the Temple, "O God, pardon those who caused my parents to die!"

Presently Madame de Gontaut arrived from the Elysée, bringing with her the infant Princess, daughter of the Duc and Duchesse de Berry, her father having expressed a wish to embrace her once more. "Poor child!" said he to her; "poor child! I trust that thou mayst be less unfortunate than my family generally!"

Respiration was now becoming difficult to the dying Prince, and he was therefore conveyed from the small salon at the back of the Royal box to the Opera *Salle d'Administration.* A bed was arranged for him there, and it was necessary to borrow the furniture of pleasure to supply necessaries for this bed of death. A painful operation was then performed: the wound was enlarged to compel the blood to flow afresh and more freely, as there was danger of suffocation. The royal patient's father tried in vain to draw away his daughter-in-law from her husband's side, for he dreaded her witnessing the agony caused by this operation; but it was impossible to detach her from him. "My father," said she, "do not force me to disobey you!" Then, turning to the surgeon, "Sir," she continued, "act; I will not interrupt you; act!" Her tears flowed with the blood of her husband, as kneeling by his side she held his left hand. At last he spoke again: "You suffer for love of me; my poor wife, you are unfortunate!" And he lovingly passed his hand through her hair. Then, seeing her anguish increase as his strength decreased, he added, in a louder and firmer voice, "My love, do not allow yourself to be overwhelmed by grief; take care of yourself for the sake of the child that you carry near your heart."

At these words an electric thrill passed through all that heard them. The Royalists assembled there could not conceal the intense interest they felt in them. At the side of this opening tomb a cradle had appeared!

The Duc de Berry had frequently asked questions concerning his assassin. "What have I ever done to this man? Have I unintentionally offended him?"—"No," answered Monsieur. "You, my son, have never seen him."—"Then he is a madman?" suggested the dying Prince, adding, "The King comes not. I shall not have time to implore him to pardon this man."

It was two o'clock in the morning, the Prince was sinking fast, and the offices of religion were soon to be administered to him. Suddenly, the Duc de Berry, feeling that his last hour was approaching, expressed to the Princess, his wife, who knelt beside him, his desire once more to behold and embrace the two children who were his by that *liaison*, before mentioned, which had been sanctioned during his exile in England, but which had never been solemnized by the religion, nor legalised by the family to which he belonged.

"Where are they?" asked the Duchesse de Berry. "Where are these children? I will be their mother."

In three-quarters of an hour afterwards the children entered—two graceful little girls, who, suddenly disturbed from their slumbers in that home in which their father had in some sort continued to exercise surveillance over them, wept as they now approached the bed where, pale and bleeding, he lay dying.

The Duchesse de Berry herself went forward to meet them, and led them to her husband; then she presented her own little daughter to them, saying, "Embrace your sister." Afterwards she bent down again towards her husband and said to him repeatedly—"Charles, Charles, I have three children now."

A voice from behind the bed exclaimed—"She is sublime!" It was Madame Royale, Duchesse d'Angoulême, who spoke. None could better appreciate this noble conduct on the part of her young sister-in-law than she, the daughter of the martyred King, who herself manifested self-abnegation when not four years before she lovingly received this Princess, who then came as her rival, but whom from that time forth she had adopted as a daughter.

About three o'clock in the morning the Duc de Berry began to suffer the last agonies of death, and the ministers of religion approached his pillow. He listened to the exhortations of the Bishop de Chartres, and rallied strength sufficient to make his confession aloud, to pray audibly to God for pardon, and to entreat those around him to forgive him any offence he might have caused them, or any scandal which his example might have afforded. The Curé of Saint Roch brought the sacred oils, and the consolations of religion seemed so far to mitigate and soothe the agony of the Prince, that the Duchesse de Berry, in a momentary exaltation of anguish, cried out—"Ah! I knew well that his soul was born for Heaven, and that it would return thither."

Severe sufferings intervened ere its release. "This night is long," said the dying man. And when the Marshals arrived he murmured—"Upon the field of battle would I have wished to die, in the midst of you."

At last came the King. The Duc de Berry then rallied his whole remaining strength to implore pardon for his murderer. But the King evaded these entreaties. He said to his nephew, the sight of whose agonies affected the aged Monarch very deeply: "My son, you will recover. We will speak again of what you ask. Let us think now but of you."

Once the Prince murmured—"The man's pardon might nevertheless have soothed my last moments." His last words were—"Oh, my country! Unhappy France!"

Thus, like his ancestor Henri IV., perished by the hand of an assassin, Charles Ferdinand d'Artois, Duc de Berry; and it is to one of the stanchest adherents of the ancient race to which he belonged that I am indebted for many of the particulars I have here given of his last moments.

CHAPTER XV.

EXECUTION OF THE ASSASSIN LOUVEL — REMOVAL OF THE DUCHESSE DE BERRY TO THE TUILERIES — ST. DENIS — ROSNY — BIRTH OF (HENRY V.) COMTE DE CHAMBORD — RENEWED GAIETIES AT PARIS — MISS B—— AT THE OPERA — CAPTAIN G——, R.N. — BALL AT THE BRITISH EMBASSY — CURIOUS ELOPEMENT — MR. W——'S WIGS — LADY B—— AT VERSAILLES — PAYMENT *v.* PRONUNCIATION.

CHAPTER XV.

THERE had been some fear of alarming the King by the intelligence that his nephew was stabbed; but when it was found that the sharp blade of the dagger (six inches long) had penetrated the breast of the Prince to such a depth that no doubt could be entertained of the fatal nature of the wound, the King was aroused from sleep, and too soon learnt that his nephew, whom he called his "son," and whose conversation had so much amused him not many hours previously, was about "to rejoin Henri IV., Louis XVI., and the Duc d'Enghien."

It seemed a long time before the King came, but, nevertheless, he said when aroused—"Let us start." He was assisted to rise, and despite all representations of the Duc de Châtres and others in attendance on him, as to the baneful effect of the effort on his own health, he lost no time in proceeding from the Tuileries to the scene of death, through the streets, in which his subjects were still merry-making in the enjoyment of the Carnival. They knew not that it was the King's carriage which, illumined by torch-bearers, passed through the crowd at that hour of the night, or rather of the morning; and still less did the majority of the masqueraders suspect that it was to witness the death of their favourite Prince, His Majesty was wending his way.

When the day had fully dawned, and the fatal intelligence was announced, the consternation was general, and Lent, as declares a French chronicler, then began in earnest.

Was Louvel, the assassin of the Duc de Berry, a fanatic, or the agent of some secret conspiracy?

That became the question, and none were able to answer it but by all sorts of conjectures. Ministerial vigilance, and the activity of the police in attempting to solve this question, only excited party-feeling afresh, and helped to provoke public uneasiness as to political results.

The assassin himself denied that he was the

tool of any conspiracy, and to suspect in this case was to calumniate. Louvel manifested, or affected, a fanatical glory in his crime, and, in answer to interrogatories, declared that, after having killed the Duc de Berry, he had intended to kill the King, Monsieur, and the Duc d'Angoulême. In his regicide politics and atheistical philosophy, he belonged to the revolutionary school of the last decade of the last century.

The premature announcement in London and elsewhere of the death of the Duc de Berry was remembered, now that that event had really taken place, as a proof of conspiracy. The criminal must have had confidants if he had not accomplices.

Be this as it may, he was executed, and surmises of his secret alone survived him. Until the last he maintained an arrogant demeanour, which impressed some who observed him with the idea that he expected deliverance. He became so faint, however, as he approached the scaffold, that it was necessary to carry him up the ascent to it. He was unconscious before he died, and thus made no last dying speech or confession.

The King remained at the Tuileries. The unhappy widow of the murdered Prince was soon conveyed to St. Cloud, where nothing but the hope that she was about again to become a mother, as her husband in his last hours had proclaimed, rescued her from despair. She remembered that his hand had rested on her head, and been entwined with her hair in his latest moments, and to that memory she made the sacrifice of those flowing locks—that *belle chevelure qu'il aimait tant.* In time she was removed to the Tuileries, to that part of the Château called the Pavillon Marsan, where she remained in seclusion, but soothed as far as possible by the affection of her father-in-law, Monsieur, the Comte d'Artois, and by the ministrations of her brother and sister-in-law, the Duc and Duchesse d'Angoulême.

In another part of the palace the King had asked Madame de Cayla if she remembered the prediction of Martin—"From death life shall spring." His sorrow at the fulfilment of one portion of this prophecy made the King hope that the other would be realised; but still shaken and depressed by the death of his nephew, His Majesty added, whilst conversing with his confidante—

"I find myself regretting the solitude and abandonment of my exile. Ah! could I have believed that the land of France had such bitter fruits in reserve for me!" And then the King anxiously asked himself, "Ought we to have inflicted ourselves on the French? Will a revolution bring forth new regicides?"

But Madame de Cayla answered—"Ah, Sire, the death we deplore was the act of a madman. There is no conspiracy, no revolution, which menaces you. A general stupor prevails."

"Nevertheless," replied the King, "a cruel fatality is implacable towards our house; and, since forty years past, the Prince de Condé, then lately dead, is the only one whose end has not been hastened by violence or extraordinary means."

Madame Royale accompanied Louis XVIII. to St. Denis, there to attend the funeral of her brother-in-law, the Duc de Berry. The vaults, sacred to the ancient Royalty of France for centuries, which had been desecrated during the Revolution, and to which, on January 15, had been transferred the bones of Louis XVI., were now re-opened to receive the mortal remains of the youngest Prince of his house—the only one through whom there had been, and still were, hopes of the perpetuation of his race.

Like that of his ancestor, Henri IV., the body of the Duc de Berry had lain in state at the Louvre until the 22nd of February. All France had resorted thither, either to satisfy curiosity or to evince sympathy and respect; but when the mortal remains of the Prince were transferred to St. Denis crowds of the poor who regarded him as a benefactor, voluntarily joined the funeral cortége on foot, "and not even the eulogistic and elegiac biography, shortly afterwards published by M. de Châteaubriand, of the Duc de Berry, was so eloquent in his praise, as were the tears and lamentations of those whose wants he had munificently relieved, and who mourned him as their best friend."

The 14th of March was the day appointed by the King for the funeral service to be performed at St. Denis; but the magnificence with which it was conducted did not lessen the woe of those who attended. The Duc d'Angoulême descended into the vault before the coffin of his brother was lowered into it, that he might be there to receive it. The solemn time at which he did so was marked by the firing of twenty-one guns. At the moment when the body-guards of Monsieur—father of the deceased—silently raised the coffin to help to carry it with slow steps towards the vault, the Duchesse d'Angoulême first knelt down as it passed, but her sorrow was so overpowering that she was obliged to retire. She who had been so severely tried in the cruel school of affliction, that she had no smiles nor tears for ordinary occasions, was still at heart as sensitive as when she fainted at her father's feet on the night before his execution. She inherited the sensibility of her mother, Marie Antoinette, but adversity and solitary imprisonment in early years had made her reserved.

The King, by whose side she was placed until compelled to withdraw, was also much affected. Tears flowed from his eyes, but the tears of old men are not always painful, as are those of reticent women who, like the Duchesse d'Angoulême, dread to shed them in public. The Dowager Duchesse d'Orléans, with her son Louis Philippe and his wife, was present at St. Denis on that day. Also the Duc de Bourbon, who had never ceased to mourn the untimely death of the Duc d'Enghien.

The funeral oration was pronounced by M. de Quélen, coadjutor of the Archbishop of Paris. French chronicles of the *ancien régime* abound with minute particulars of solemnities due to the sad occasion. The lofty interior of St. Denis was hung with black, illumined by thousands of lights, "which shone like ropes of fire against the dense background." The whole scene, the solemn occasion of it, the sight of the Royal Family in profound sorrow, the words of the preacher, and the strains of sacred music mingling with audible sobs, as "the grandeur of earth prostrated itself before the majesty of the coffin," impressed all beholders, and inspired them with fresh loyalty towards the Crown. The seclusion of the Duchesse de Berry was too much respected for any intrusion as yet to have been made on it, although it was now essential to ascertain her wishes with regard to the disposal of the heart of her husband, which, temporarily, had been deposited at St. Denis by the Bishop of

Amiens. But her answer was prompt; she had already resolved to consecrate her Château of Rosny by the construction of a chapel there. At Rosny, where with her husband she had enjoyed the privacy of domestic life, and where she had passed many days of happiness, now gone from her for ever, she desired to enshrine the relic most dear to her.

"My intentions are fixed," she said. "I am about to cause a building to be erected at Rosny,—a pavilion with two wings. In one, the sick will be cared for; in the other, poor children. The centre will be a chapel, where prayers to God will be offered up for my husband."

There was great political uneasiness in France during the next few months; in Spain and Naples the revolutionary spirit had again declared itself. Royalists in France looked forward to the advent of a Prince, with confident hope that the lineal descendant of Henri IV. could not fail to be popular from the hour of his birth; and about three in the morning of the 29th of September, a Prince was born. Dreading suspicions, the Duchesse de Berry herself took measures, with the aid of her medical attendant, that the event should be verified beyond even what the law on such Royal occasions demanded; and when her ladies—Mesdames de Reggio and Gontaut—entered her chamber, she exclaimed with rapture, which was pathetic in contrast to her woe of widowhood,—"It is Henri!"

The Duchesse d'Angoulême was one of the first to congratulate her sister-in-law in not only possessing a blessing which had been denied to her, but in the increase of personal consideration such a possession would bring with it. Monsieur, with the Duc and Duchesse d'Angoulême, had entered before the King arrived; but when His Majesty did come he was neither empty-handed nor slow of speech. "God be praised!" said he to the Duchesse de Berry, "you have a son." She held her hand towards him; and in it Louis XVIII. placed a superb bouquet of diamonds. "This is for you," said he. Then, taking the new-born babe in his arms, he added, with emotion—"And *this* is for me." Then, according to an ancient Béarnais custom, His Majesty took a clove of garlic and some old Tarançon wine; with the former he rubbed the lips of the babe, and dropped some of the latter into his mouth. The child sustained these tests better than might have been expected; and the mother exclaimed,—"Sire, I should like to know the air of the Song of Jeanne d'Albret, that everything might happen here as it did at the birth of Henri IV."

News of the joyous event at the Tuileries spread like wildfire through Paris. Twenty-four cannon were fired; and, by six in the morning, a crowd of people, eager to offer congratulations, had assembled under the windows of the Duchesse de Berry. The different members of the Royal Family resident at the Tuileries had been summoned so hastily, that they were only half-dressed when they appeared in the chamber of the Prince just born to them; but as the crowd increased in the gardens below, some recognition from within was felt to be necessary. Meantime, the people distinctly recognised the Duchesse d'Angoulême passing and re-passing the windows above, as she was occupied in attending on her sister-in-law, who had just presented the nation with the Prince, of whom she herself had once hoped to be the mother. Who can declare what sadness mingled with the joy that this event brought to the childless Duchesse d'Angoulême! If the child calmly sleeping its first sleep in the cradle over which she watched, had but been her own, how different might have been the fate of that child, of France, and of herself!

Old soldiers were the first strangers who visited the infant descendant of Henri IV. One of them—an old grenadier—who, during the Revolution, had fought bravely in La Vendée, audibly blessed the babe, and vowed by his cradle to give six more years of his services to France.

Another old soldier, covered with wounds, began to lament the decrepitude which past glory had brought to him. "Ah, my Prince!" cried he, "Why am I old and disabled? I shall not serve beneath your orders!"

At half-past nine, the Orléans family came to congratulate the Duchesse de Berry, and at eleven the King held a grand reception in the salons of the Tuileries. The throng was so great that His Majesty, Monsieur (grandfather of the infant Prince), and the Duc and Duchesse d'Angoulême, with other members of the Royal Family, had difficulty in passing through the ranks of loyal subjects, on their way to the Chapel, where thanks were offered up for the blessing just vouchsafed to France.

On his way back from mass, the King presented himself, surrounded by his family, to the crowd of his subjects assembled outside the Tuileries. He stood on the central balcony of the Château; loud acclamations greeted him; he made a sign that he wished to address the multitude, and then Louis XVIII. said, while a sudden and solemn silence prevailed:—"My friends, your joy increases mine a hundredfold. A child is born to us all. This child will, one day, become your father; he will love you as I love you, and as you love all who belong to me."

The joyous shouts from the crowd outside the palace were heard by the Duchesse de Berry; she longed herself to present her infant son to the people of France; she felt that no other protection now was left to her fatherless child; and, much to the consternation of her medical attendants, she insisted on her bed being wheeled to one of the windows of her chamber, that she might see her son's future subjects, and be seen by them with him in her arms. Her solicitations to those around her were too ardent to be resisted, and all was done as she desired. Twice she raised herself from a recumbent position, and held up her child in view of the multitude, whose whole interest thus became concentrated on the window at which she displayed herself. But the effort was too great; the excitement too intense. She was seized with faintness, and medical assistance soon became necessary. The enthusiastic shouts of the people still rang in her ears, and it was thought advisable to administer an opiate to her; but she put it away from her, saying, as she once more bowed to the crowd—*Merci! Ce bruit-là est le meilleur calmant!*

Soon after the birth of Henri, Duc de Bordeaux (now called by legitimists Henri V., and by the world at large, Count de Chambord), a protest appeared in a number of the *Morning Chronicle*, which threw doubt on his being really the son of the Duc and Duchesse de Berry. This number of the *Morning Chronicle* reached the Tuileries. Louis XVIII., not knowing to whom to attribute the article, which excited his utmost indignation, became unjust and suspicious in his wrath; so that when the Duc d'Orléans, who had also read it, presented himself before him, he was received with cold severity by His Majesty. But the Duc d'Orléans eagerly justified himself. The Marshal d'Albugera was one of those who attested the fact of the birth, and of him the Duc d'Orléans had asked,—"Is Madame the Duchesse de Berry really the mother of a Prince?" To which the Marshal had replied,—"As certainly as Your Highness is father of the Duc de Chartres!" And the Duc d'Orléans had then declared himself satisfied;—as, also, was the King with the explanation of the Duc d'Orléans.

After the birth of the Duc de Bordeaux, Paris resumed a gay aspect. The Italian Opera, where only a few months ago the tragic scene, already described, had taken place, was frequented as much as formerly; and balls at the various Embassies succeeded each other.

Shortly before this I often met Lord and Lady B——. Their daughter, the Hon.

Ann B——, a beautiful girl about nineteen years of age, was under vigilant chaperonage.

Nevertheless one night when we went together to the Opera, Captain (since Admiral) G—— was of our party. He was by no means young, and Miss B—— used to laugh at him immoderately. An old sailor ashore, his dress, like his manners, was somewhat peculiar, and she "quizzed" him excessively, even to his square-toed shoes.

Sometimes she was taken to task for this, as he was a relation of her mother's; and Lady B—— had such confidence in him that she sent him everywhere in attendance upon her daughter, with strict injunctions to watch every person to whom she spoke, and to note all the partners with whom she danced.

The night just mentioned, when Miss B—— and I were both at the Opera, Captain G—— would have seated himself next to her, had she not requested me to prevent his so doing, and that in a way so earnest that I was more than ever convinced of her dislike to him. The next night we went to a ball at the English Embassy; and Miss B——, who was much admired, still continued to manifest her distaste to the family friend and gallant officer who was deputed to observe her movements. Mr. and Mrs. Drummond were not at that time in Paris; we were all staying at Versailles, but my father came with us to Paris. It happened, therefore, when the ball was over at a late hour of the night, or rather at an early one in the morning, that my father and Lord B—— conducted us to the hotel in Paris where apartments had been engaged for us, and where Mr. and Mrs. W——, —an English lady and gentleman, who had also been to the Embassy ball—were staying.

Tired with dancing, I soon fell into a profound sleep; but about seven o'clock I was suddenly awakened by somebody knocking at my door, and asking for Miss B——. I answered that she was not in my room, but that the one she occupied was close at hand.

I was then told to open my door, and recognising the voice as Mrs. W——'s, I obeyed as quickly as I could throw a dressing-gown around me. And truly there seemed no time to be lost, for when Mrs. W—— stood face to face with me, she was in such an evident state of agitation that I too was seized with a panic of alarm concerning Miss B——.

"She is gone," cried Mrs. W——; "she is gone. Her maid went as usual into her room this morning, but no Miss B—— was there. She has left no explanation of her absence, and she is nowhere to be found."

I was thunderstruck; but the question instantly suggested itself, "With whom had she gone?" For of course it was not to be supposed that Miss B——, the daughter of indulgent parents, had eloped alone.

"With whom had she gone?"

One by one Mrs. W—— helped me to enumerate all the most distinguished or dangerous-looking men with whom Miss B—— had danced the preceding night at the Embassy; but we failed in selecting an object for our suspicions to fix upon.

Lord B——, meantime, was running frantically through the hotel, and demanding news of his missing daughter in most unlikely quarters. But where was Captain G——? Where was that family friend whose age and discretion had caused him to be trusted as the most safe and vigilant guardian of the young lady? Where was he? Just as this question was mooted, and when Lord B—— was in sore need of his friend's help, it was reported that an ostler belonging to the hotel had some information to give regarding the subject of our inquiry.

The ostler was called; he seemed somewhat confused, but at last he made a clear enough declaration, to the effect, that about six o'clock that morning, Captain G——, having previously ordered his carriage, had come down from his rooms, and had driven off with a young lady who had made her appearance about the same time.

Directly Lord B—— heard this, he, my father, and Mr. W—— started in pursuit of the fugitives as fast as horses could carry them; and knowing not which road to take, they proceeded by different routes, so as to make inquiries along every main suburban thoroughfare. My father and Lord B—— went in one direction, and Mr. W—— in another, and not many hours had elapsed before every barrier-keeper round Paris was questioned as to what travellers had passed that morning, but all to no purpose; and this, not for lack of information, but the contrary, for *each* gatekeeper declared that a carriage containing an elderly gentleman and a young lady had passed, so that it was impossible to identify the one which had whirled away Miss B—— and her mature admirer.

While these inquiries were being prosecuted, I remained with Mrs. W——, she being, like myself, in a state of great anxiety. Yet it is sometimes strange how, in such a state of mind a sudden sense of the ridiculous, awakened by some trifling circumstance, flashes through more serious thoughts; for while we were both standing opposite Mr. W——'s dressing-room, the door of which, in the haste of his departure, had been left open, I perceived a gentleman's wig hanging there, and inquired of Mrs. W—— to whom it could possibly belong, for Mr. W—— was the last man I suspected of wearing one. She burst out laughing at my question, and in reply to it exclaimed, "For goodness' sake, don't let him know; pray, never say that I told you, but that wig belongs to my husband. Nor that alone; for he has four in all—one with very short hair, as if it had just been cut; one with very long hair, as if it wanted cutting; another with the hair moderately long, as if it had grown since cutting; and one elaborately dressed for parties. Sometimes," she added, "I can scarcely prevent myself from laughing, when I hear an intimate friend advise him to go and get his hair cut, and perceive how, by change of wig, it is supposed that such advice has been promptly taken."

I was surprised as well as amused at the moment of this discovery concerning a "dandy" of the time of "the first gentleman of Europe;" but the amusement was quickly overpowered by the anxiety that beset us—an anxiety which was combined with another—when presently Lord B——, my father, and Mr. W—— returned from their equally fruitless journeys; for Lady B——, as already said, was at Versailles, whither that evening we were compelled to return, and how was the intelligence of her daughter's elopement to be broken to her?

We might, however, have spared ourselves all solicitude on this point. When we reached Versailles, Lady B—— was prepared to give us the information which we had elsewhere sought in vain, for a letter had been received by her from her daughter, stating that she had gone off with Captain G——, and that she was instantly to be married to him. And, strange to say, Lady B—— was by no means dissatisfied, for, like not a few British matrons of her time, she had dreaded the possibility of her daughter marrying a Frenchman, or a penniless officer of any nation; and Captain G——, if he had neither much youth nor beauty, had plenty of money.

Besides all this, my fugitive friend's mother had other anxieties, one of which ought to be a warning to English travellers when they attempt to make good bargains abroad.

Lady B—— exhibited to us a quantity of beautiful Malines lace, the purchase of which she had effected, amongst others, during our absence in Paris. The lace had been delivered to her; the other purchases had not. The lace she thought magnificent, but too yellow; and she at once ordered her maid to plunge it into boiling soap and water. From this ordeal, or bath, the lace came out white enough, and Lady B——, now quite content with her acquisition, thought that she had indeed made a good bargain; for, as she believed, she had only promised to pay for it *cinq* (five) francs a yard.

With the next morning, however, came the lace-vendor, and forthwith handed to Lady B—— a bill for the lace at *cent* (a hundred) francs a yard. The unfortunate purchaser looked at the bill in horror, and then began to dispute it. But her remonstrances had no effect; it was a mere question of pronunciation. The French lace-vendor volubly, but distinctly, demonstrated that *cinq* was not *cent*, but still was willing to take back the lace, which, after all, even at a hundred instead of five francs a yard, had been parted with, a bargain. The lace was brought forth by the maid, but only to elicit a fresh explosion of indignation and anger on the part of the lace-seller; for it was no longer of the yellow tint so much desired by connoisseurs, but white! As to taking back the lace in *that* state, no Frenchwoman who knew how to blend the tints of her wares with those of their wearers could think of so doing. And it was flung back in disdain on the hands of

Lady B——, who, in case of resistance, was threatened by a visit from the huissiers.

So, although she had lost her daughter, she was obliged to keep her lace, which would have made no inappropriate present for the bride; but whether or not such an idea occurred to her, I cannot say.

END OF THE FIRST VOLUME.

CPSIA information can be obtained
at www.ICGtesting.com
Printed in the USA
LVHW112015030423
743357LV00006B/548